# A Sinister Silence

# A Sinister Silence

Jane Peart

Fleming H. Revell
A Division of Baker Book House Co
Grand Rapids, Michigan 49516

Published by Fleming H. Revell
a division of Baker Book House Company
P.O. Box 6287, Grand Rapids, MI 49516-6287

Printed in the United States of America

**Library of Congress Cataloging-in-Publication Data**

Peart, Jane.
    A sinister silence / Jane Peart.
        p.    cm.—(Edgecliffe Manor mysteries)
    ISBN 0-8007-5763-7
    1. Inheritance and succession—Fiction. 2. Deaf—Fiction.
I. Title.
PS3566.E238 S58 2001
813'.54—dc21                        2001034952

For current information about all releases from Baker Book House, visit our web site:
                http://www.bakerbooks.com

# Prologue

## Mallory Hall

### *1896*

*P*aige woke up with a start, not knowing what had awakened her. She was lying in her canopied bed in her own room. Everything seemed the same, yet something was different. Why did she feel so strange?

Puzzled, she struggled to raise herself on her elbows, but the effort was too great. She fell back upon the pillows. Why was she so weak? What had happened? Had she been in an accident? Fallen from her horse?

She turned her head toward the bedroom window. Outside, a fierce wind tossed the bare oak tree branches, scraping them on the glass. Rain pelted the latticed panes. Why couldn't she hear the noise of the storm?

Slowly she realized there was no sound in the room either. Not the crackle of the logs brightly burning in the fireplace, nor the tick of her small French clock on the mantelpiece. Its hands pointed to four, but no musical chimes marked the hour.

Something was terribly wrong. What was it?

Flora would know; *she* would explain. Paige reached for the silver bell on the bedside table to ring for her maid. She couldn't hear its jingle. She shook it furiously until the bell spun out of her grasp and onto the floor. "Flora!" she called again and again. But she could not hear her own voice. Terrified now, she felt her throat muscles contract as she frantically screamed the name "Flora!"

Within seconds the bedroom door flew open and Flora rushed in and over to the bedside. Suddenly the room was full of people. First came Dr. Grantly, the family physician, followed by Paige's grandmother Lady Ursula Mallory and her sister, Great-aunt Enid. Next Demetra Colfax, Paige's cousin, slipped in behind them. Lastly Thatcher, Paige's closest friend from childhood, brushed by the others and bent over her, taking her hand in both of his.

Paige grasped them. "Thatcher, what's wrong with me? I can't hear anything!"

He glanced quickly at Dr. Grantly standing nearby. The doctor took a small pad out of his vest pocket and wrote on it, then held it up for Paige to read. *You have been very ill for nearly a month. Due to the high fever, you have suffered a temporary loss of hearing.*

Paige shook her head, protesting. "No, no, no!" It was only then she became aware of her fiancé, Charles Bennett, standing at the foot of the bed. He was regarding her with an expression of bewilderment and anxiety. As she met his gaze, memory flooded back. "Our wedding! Oh, Charles, we were to be married on New Year's Day. . . ."

Dr. Grantly scribbled on the pad again. *Postponed.*

*Nearly a month.* Paige read the doctor's words again in disbelief, then looked at Charles. "Oh, Charles," she moaned, "I'm so sorry."

The others turned toward Charles, and Thatcher stepped away so that her fiancé could take his place at the bedside. Paige longed for Charles to take her in his arms and comfort her, to express his own distress and disappointment at what had happened. But that would be unlike Charles, ever the disciplined soldier. Yet she knew there were things they might have said to each other in private that couldn't be said in front of the others.

A whole month! Lost! It was 1896, and she hadn't even seen the new year's arrival. Paige's heart ached realizing she and Charles should have been on their Italian honeymoon. It was all too dreadful. Tears flowed down her cheeks.

Charles drew back, then cast an anxious glance at the doctor, who leaned over her again.

Dr. Grantly wrote on his pad and held it up. *Now, you must not get upset, young lady. Weeping will only make things worse. If you are to get well, you must rest.*

But she couldn't. He was trying to calm her, but the truth was too devastating. She looked at all the faces surrounding the bed. Aunt Enid and cousin Demetra had come especially for her wedding; Demetra, at her grandmother's insistence, to be included as a member of the bridal party. And they were still here. Paige now remembered all the preparations—the flowers, the gowns, the lavish reception to be held at the ancestral home, Mallory Hall. All for nothing . . .

She couldn't remember getting sick. It must have been sudden. Her head throbbed. Everything was a blur.

Dr. Grantly motioned for everyone to leave, and one by one they filed out. Paige would have liked Charles to stay, but his military training had taught him to follow orders, and he left with the others.

Only Thatcher lingered. Paige clung to his hand. They had been through so much together growing up as orphans at Mallory Hall. Certainly he could help her understand. However, when Dr. Grantly gave him an impatient look, Thatcher leaned down and kissed her cheek, then grabbed the pad from the bedside table and wrote furiously. *Courage, Mopsy. All will be well.* Mopsy—his childhood nickname for her because of her unruly dark curls. He squeezed her hand again, then hesitated a moment before he, too, left the room.

Flora, backed against the wall, obviously trying to make herself inconspicuous, remained.

Dr. Grantly put his face close to Paige's and slowly mouthed something she assumed was meant to be reassuring. However, Paige was too distraught to accept his compassionate attempt. All she knew was that she was deaf, and no one knew for how long. Her wedding was postponed and with it all her hopes and dreams for the future.

Marriage to Charles was to have been her escape from Mallory Hall's oppressive atmosphere and from her grandmother's thinly veiled dislike. Now she was trapped—enveloped in a silence that was deep, smothering, and somehow sinister.

Wearily Paige closed her eyes and prayed that she might wake up and find all of this a nightmare.

*A*s Paige drifted in and out of her sedative-induced slumber, a series of scenes, like images on a magic-lantern screen, passed before her . . .

It was the morning of the rehearsal party two days before the wedding, a blustery December day with cold rain turning rapidly into sleet. The weather, however, did not deter Paige from going out, accompanied by Demetra, for some last-minute shopping. Their first stop was the jeweler's to pick up Charles's gift. She had left it to be engraved a few days before.

When she had first selected the silver watch fob, she had asked the clerk to engrave a particular Shakespeare quotation on the back. But as she was quoting it and the clerk was writing it down, Demetra shyly tapped Paige's arm.

"Excuse me," she said in a low voice, "but I think that's incorrect. Shouldn't it be 'love is not love which alters when it alteration finds'?"

Paige hesitated.

The clerk nodded. "I believe the young lady is right, Miss Mallory." He seemed a little embarrassed.

Paige had simply laughed. "Correct it, then."

"You're not offended, are you, Paige?" Demetra asked doubtfully.

"Of course not. You were always smarter than me, Demetra," she said, recalling their early school days together with their governess, Miss Boles, when Demetra still lived at Mallory Hall.

Paige was so happy that nothing bothered her. Certainly not her cousin's tactful rescue from a mistake that Charles would have noticed himself.

They completed a few other errands, then headed back to the parish church for the wedding rehearsal. After that they would return home to prepare for the gala evening ahead.

When Paige came up to her bedroom to dress for the ball, Flora looked at her abnormally bright eyes and flushed cheeks and clucked her tongue. "You look feverish, miss. You shouldna' gone out in this nasty weather; it'll be a wonder if you don't catch your death of cold."

"I'm fine, just excited," Paige assured her.

Still shaking her head, Flora helped Paige into her gold satin gown shimmering with tiny beads. Paige was sitting alone at her dressing table, fastening a glittering ornamental comb in her hair, when a light tap came at the bedroom door. Demetra's quiet voice asked, "Paige, may I come in?"

"Of course." Paige watched her cousin's reflection in the mirror as she approached, thinking that Demetra had grown into an attractive young woman in contrast to the rather plain little girl she had once been. When they had been children together at Mallory Hall, Demetra had never taken part in any of the childish pranks Thatcher and Paige delighted in. In fact, she had seemed to take perverse pleasure in reporting their mischief to Miss Boles, as well as enjoying the resulting punishment they received. Thatcher and Paige had reciprocated mainly by ignoring Demetra. They didn't even miss her when, abruptly and inexplicably, she and her parents disappeared from Mallory Hall. Neither Paige nor

Thatcher had seen Demetra again until she had arrived for the wedding festivities.

She was prettier than Paige would have expected, with porcelain skin, hair the color of polished maple, and hazel eyes. The triangular shape of her face reminded Paige of a kitten. There the illusion ended, for Demetra lacked a kitten's playful charm. Her demeanor was demure, and only the firmness of her chin indicated the stubbornness of character that might lie underneath the surface. To be fair, Paige conceded, Demetra must have had to acquire a certain reserve in her employment as a governess. After all, she was only a year older than Paige, yet she had been deprived by circumstances of the same kind of carefree life Paige enjoyed.

"Your gown is beautiful, Paige. Mine is—" She hesitated. "I just hope I don't look dreadfully dowdy in contrast."

Immediately Paige was struck with guilt. Of course, a governess's salary did not provide money for ball gowns.

"Not at all. With your complexion and eyes, you look lovely in whatever you wear." Impulsively, she started to offer Demetra the pick of any of the dresses in her armoire. Then she realized none would fit because she was taller by inches than her cousin. What she could do was offer Demetra a choice of jewelry from her mother's stunning collection, which she had inherited. Any jewel would do to accessorize Demetra's simple, gray taffeta dress.

She opened the box on top of her dressing table. "Here, choose something you'd like to wear, Demetra. The coral and pearls would be perfect with your dress."

Demetra's eyes brightened, then she drew back. "Oh, I couldn't!"

"You must! Please. I insist."

Demetra began to look carefully through the assortment of lovely pieces. After some consideration, she selected a choker of freshwater pearls and coral beads. When it was clasped around her neck and the matching pendant earrings were fastened in her delicate ears, it created the perfect effect.

"Here, take this fan as well." Paige handed her the gilt and lace fan she had intended to carry herself.

"Oh, thank you, Paige. Now I do feel grand."

A knock sounded at the door. "Ready, Paige?" It was Thatcher, come to escort her downstairs.

"Coming!" Paige said, and Demetra went to open the door.

Thatcher, splendid in evening clothes, made a bow. "Don't you ladies both look beautiful?"

Demetra blushed and gave a little responding bow, then brushed past him. Thatcher's glance followed the departing figure, then came inside the room.

"Borrowed finery, I assume?" He seemed amused. "The moth has certainly turned into a butterfly, hasn't she?"

"Yes, and she's changed in other ways as well," Paige replied. "Quite pretty, don't you think? Remember we used to call her 'Mouse'?" She giggled. "We were awful, weren't we?" Then she twirled around, holding out the train of her gown. "So, what do you think of me?"

"A stunner, as the Pre-Raphaelite artists would say."

"Thank you, sir. And you look very handsome yourself. If I weren't engaged, I might be smitten, as surely as all the young ladies will be at the sight of you tonight!"

"And you, miss, look so enchanting I could challenge Charles to a duel for your hand."

Paige laughed. She and Thatcher had a rare kind of camaraderie; they had bonded in childhood when they had both come to live at Mallory Hall. While Lady Ursula was Paige's grandmother, Thatcher was not related at all. He was Lady Ursula's ward, however, the son of dear friends of hers, his father a comrade of her brother.

As Paige took Thatcher's arm and they proceeded down the curved stairway, she gazed up at him with admiration. Thatcher *was* exceptionally good-looking—tall, well built, with thick, wavy dark hair. His features were strong yet aristocratic, his gray eyes thoughtful but with a hint of humor.

When they reached the bottom step, Paige saw that the party had already begun. Her grandmother's disapproving glance made her realize she was late taking her place in the receiving line. The first guests had already arrived. Paige was used to being the object of her grandmother's disapproval, but tonight she was determined not to let anything spoil her pleasure.

"There's your toy-soldier boy," Thatcher whispered teasingly.

Paige felt her heart turn over. Involuntarily, she drew in her breath and squeezed Thatcher's arm. Charles looked magnificent in his dress uniform, brilliant red tunic, and gleaming gold braid. His fair hair was smoothed back from his broad forehead, and his newly acquired mustache added a certain panache to his appearance.

At that same moment, Charles caught sight of them. He excused himself from the group with whom he was chatting and came across the room. He bowed and spoke to Lady Ursula, then held out his hand to Paige.

As she glided into Charles's arms and out onto the polished floor, Paige knew she had never been so happy in all her life. She felt light-headed, floating in a cloud of pure joy.

"You are sparkling tonight, did you know?" Charles asked.

"I am delirious." Paige smiled. "In two days we'll be married and on our way to Italy for our honeymoon. I am the happiest, luckiest girl in the world."

Charles was a superb dancer. They circled the room in perfect rhythm. As they whirled by Demetra, Paige saw that her expression was wistful. At once she was struck by the unfairness of their different situations. She had everything, while Demetra had very little.

"You must dance with Demetra," Paige said quickly. "She doesn't know anyone here tonight, and she is too shy to flirt, too serious to engage anyone in small talk. Do be kind and pay her some attention."

Charles pulled a face. "I'd rather be with you."

"Please, darling. Use your charm as you do so well. Remember how you won Grandmother over? It would mean so much to me. And Demetra would be thrilled."

Charles looked resigned. "All right, my little tyrant, anything to grant your wishes."

They finished the waltz, and Paige took Charles over to hand him to Demetra.

The rest of the evening became a blur of music, candlelight, voices, and champagne. It was after midnight when at last Paige and Charles kissed good night in the windswept entry hall.

Paige stood on tiptoe and whispered into Charles's ear, "Go to the other side of the terrace under my bedroom window. I have something to give you."

With that she had run upstairs and breathlessly waited at her open window, watching for his tall, caped figure to appear. He looked up, and she lowered the tiny gift box tied on the end of a blue satin ribbon into his hands.

"I love you, Charles Bennett," she called softly.

"You are absolutely mad, Paige Mallory!" He laughed. "But I adore you."

Those were the sweetest words Paige had ever heard. Ironically, they were the last.

*O*riginally Thatcher was scheduled to leave for India after Paige's wedding. He would have been gone when she and Charles came back from their honeymoon. However, because of Paige's illness he had put off his leaving. Now that she was out of danger and getting well except for regaining her hearing, he could not delay any longer.

As his departure date drew closer, Paige dreaded his going more and more. She knew she would miss him terribly, now more than ever. During her recovery, Thatcher had spent part of every day with her. He distracted her from her problem by coaxing her to play backgammon and anagrams, writing silly puns and jokes on the notebook they passed back and forth. More importantly, he had constantly comforted and encouraged her, writing on a pad of paper, *This is only temporary, Mopsy; you're going to hear again. By the time I get back from India you'll be completely recovered.*

Without him, could she go on believing that?

"I wish you didn't have to go," she'd said over and over.

*There's no use saying that,* Thatcher wrote the last time she'd said it. *I have to go. Your toy soldier will watch over you, and*

*Aunt Ursula needs a firsthand report on how the family business is being conducted in India. She's depending on me.*

Paige understood that Thatcher felt he owed her grandmother for everything she'd given him—a home when he was orphaned, his education, and eventually a position as head of the family import firm. Still, Thatcher's absence would leave an enormous void in her life. Now especially, when she had already lost so much, to lose Thatcher, her childhood companion, confidant, and trusted friend, was almost more than she could bear.

The day Thatcher left for India, it snowed. Paige stood at her bedroom window, watching the carriage move down the driveway. From the village station Thatcher would take the train to London, then on to Liverpool. There he would board the ship *Star of India* for the long voyage.

She pressed her face against the glass pane until the coach had rounded the last bend and disappeared from sight.

With Thatcher's going, her silent world seemed more imprisoning than ever. She stared out the window at the tracks the carriage had left in the snow, then, devastated, she flung herself on her bed, weeping. Finally worn out with weeping, she fell asleep, not even fully arousing when Flora brought up her supper tray.

For days Paige remained desolate, refusing to be comforted. Then one morning about a week after Thatcher's departure she awoke to an eerie lightness in the room. She went over to the window. While she had been asleep, new snow had blanketed the ground.

Paige moved to her desk, where she picked up the silver-framed photograph of Charles. She studied the picture—his handsome face, the chiseled features, his military bearing. And then the unwanted thought came. Did Charles regret his promise to marry a bride who would now be a social liability? Before her illness they had enjoyed all the same things— riding together, dancing at his officers' club, going to plays and musicals, attending after-theater parties, and accepting other invitations. She felt a cold, clutching sensation in her heart. Charles had seemed distant and unsure how to act since her illness. Did he still love her? Or had her deafness changed his feelings?

Next to Charles's photograph was one of Thatcher. His deep-set eyes in his sensitive face seemed to look directly at her, asking, "Where's your fighting spirit, old girl? Remember, Dr. Grantly says it's only temporary. Soon you'll be right as rain."

She put down the picture, walked over to the armoire, and opened the doors. Inside, swathed in a net cover, hung her wedding dress. A marvel of design and exquisite detail in oyster white silk, the high-necked bodice had a pointed waist appliqued in scrolls of white velvet studded with tiny pearls. The overskirt was tiered to a flared hem and decorated with similar scrolled velvet. The tulle veil was attached to a wreath of jasmine and orange blossoms.

Her throat tightened. She closed the doors of the armoire and walked away. As she passed the dressing table, she caught a glimpse of herself in the mirror and halted, shocked. She hardly recognized her image. She was thin and pale, with sunken eyes shadowed by purple circles that looked like bruises. Her hair, cut off at the worst of the fever, stuck out in jagged tufts around her head and hollow face. Horrified, Paige recalled the last time she had looked in this same mirror. The image then was of a girl radiant with joy, blooming with health and the happy anticipation of the marital bliss to come.

Something drew her back to the window. She seemed to have a heightened sense of sight since her loss of hearing, and she thought she saw movement. She leaned on the sill and looked out.

Down below on the lawn, Demetra and Charles were playfully chasing each other, throwing snowballs. Even though she could not hear their voices nor the sound of their laughter, the scene wrenched her heart. It was she who should be out there frolicking with her fiancé, gaily taking part in the lighthearted fun. If only it were possible to break through that glass wall into the hearing world.

Paige clenched her teeth. "I will," she silently screamed. "Whatever it takes, I *will* get my life back."

She would start right away. Today. Tonight was none too soon.

When Flora brought in her afternoon tea tray, Paige told her she planned to dress and go downstairs for dinner.

The maid opened her mouth, probably about to say something such as, "Are you feelin' quite up to it, miss?"

To avoid the maid's protest Paige turned her back. One good thing about being deaf was that she couldn't hear what she didn't want to.

"Now don't fuss, Flora. I am getting stronger every day. And I don't want to miss this time with Charles. He has come every weekend since I was ill, and most of the time he has had to sit up here in an invalid's room. Well, there's an end to it. I'm going down to dinner like a normal person."

Flora seemed somewhat cheered by her mistress's change of attitude. She brought out two dresses and motioned for Paige to select one. Paige decided on a jade dress with soutache embroidery. The color was becoming, deepening the blue-green of her eyes. However, Paige had lost so much weight, it required some skilled pinning by Flora to make the dress fit.

Flora took special care arranging Paige's hair, making the most of its shorter length by brushing up the curls into a becoming halo around her face. A final check satisfied Paige that she looked the best she could under the circumstances.

She hurried down the steps and across the hall to the drawing room. Through the open door she saw her grandmother, Charles, and Demetra gathered about the fireplace. She stood at the door for a moment before entering. Then, taking a deep breath, she said, "Good evening, everyone. Surprise!"

They all turned around, looking startled. All three faces stared for a long moment before reacting. Then Charles rose from the sofa, where he had been sitting beside Demetra, and came over to Paige. He kissed the cheek she offered and murmured something that of course she could not hear. Lady Ursula sat as if unable to move. When she finally spoke, she wore a concerned expression, and Paige assumed she was asking her if she was well enough to be up.

"I can't remain an invalid forever," Paige replied, feeling the strangeness of her inability to hear her own voice. Was she talking too loudly? She smiled at Charles and nodded to Demetra.

She looked around. Since her deafness, Paige seemed to notice little things, things she was never aware of before. Everything was so much sharper visually. The texture of the velvet draperies, the glow of the lamplight, the gleam of the fire flickering on the brass fender. At the same time, while everything seemed more vivid, she felt as if she were viewing a scene in a stage play, as if she were not really there at all.

Paige glanced at Charles, thinking again how handsome he was and how lucky she was to be engaged to him. Thick, fair hair fell in a curving wave on his forehead. His straight nose and smooth complexion were accented by his bright blue eyes.

She had first met Charles at a riding event. Her father had placed Paige on her first pony when she was five years old, and she had grown up loving horses. Charles and Paige discovered within their first few minutes of conversation that they had a great deal in common. Charles, too, was one of those who was born to the saddle. He seemed delighted to find that such an attractive young woman shared his interest. That day began the courtship that led to their engagement.

Paige's glance moved to her cousin, Demetra. Actually, Demetra was her stepcousin. Paige's grandmother had been an impoverished young widow when she married Lord Mallory. He was twenty years her senior and had a daughter, Helena, just fifteen years younger than his new bride, Ursula. A few short months after her father's wedding, the rebellious teen had eloped with Basil Colfax. Demetra was their daughter.

Demetra looked lovely in the glow from the candlelight. Her smooth, light brown hair was drawn demurely into a high, braided coil and gleamed like polished maple. Her skin was as smooth as that of a porcelain doll. Paige had always envied her small, flared nose and her rather exotic golden-green eyes.

There had once been a long estrangement between Lady Ursula and her stepdaughter, Helena. Paige never knew what the old disagreement had been about, but Demetra had gone away as a result, and neither Helena nor Basil Colfax's names were ever spoken again. So, needless to say, Paige was surprised when her grandmother had wanted Demetra included in the bridal party.

"I've heard from Demetra several times," Lady Ursula explained. "She is governess to Lady Hadley's children now. She seems quite accomplished. I think it would be a nice change for her to come for the wedding."

That had settled it. Although Paige had not seen Demetra since they were ten years old, it was pointless to debate when Lady Ursula decided something.

Paige focused her attention from Demetra to Lady Ursula. She had once been a great beauty, but now her face was ravaged by time, tragedy, and the relentless damage of a long life of disappointment. The family fortune was eventually depleted by the excesses of the Mallory men, including her husband. Her son, Paige's father, had died, leaving no male heir. It was Paige's mother, an American heiress, whose money had saved the family estate, but this fact had not softened Lady Ursula's bitterness. Even as a child, Paige had sensed her grandmother's barely concealed dislike of her mother.

Paige had grown up knowing that her parents lived separate lives. Her mother preferred London's social scene to the isolated country estate her husband enjoyed. She was gone for months of the year and also traveled abroad. Thus Paige had become very close to her father. It was a terrible blow when he was killed in a hunting accident.

When her mother had resumed her social life only six months after Paige's father's death, Lady Ursula had referred to her sarcastically as the "merry widow." The final alienation came when Paige's mother married a Polish nobleman rich in title, poor in cash. When Paige's mother had died suddenly, Paige had been unceremoniously dumped at Mallory Hall. The Polish count was never heard from again, and Paige had remained with her grandmother.

Ten years later, Paige still felt like a stranger here. As a child, she had felt unwelcome and unwanted, and that feeling had never left. Marriage to Charles had seemed such a welcome escape.

Ironically, the one thing Paige had done that met her grandmother's approval was to agree to marry Charles. He had charmed her grandmother as much as he did every female.

Paige watched now as her grandmother gestured to Charles. He left Paige's side, set down his glass of sherry, then held out his hand to Demetra. They moved over to the piano, sat down together, and began to play a duet. Paige felt a sharp stab of pain. Once *she* and Charles had played together. Now—would she ever be able to play again? Certainly, her grandmother did not mean to be cruel. Maybe she had simply wanted to ease the awkwardness of the situation. But watching Charles and Demetra play together made Paige feel shut out.

To Paige's relief, Milton, the butler, appeared to announce dinner, and everyone moved into the dining room.

But dinner was not much better. In fact, it was interminable since Paige couldn't hear the conversation nor participate in it. When Thatcher was present, they would take delight in a lively repartee, challenging and teasing and engaging in playful arguments. He would have made sure to include her. Tonight she keenly felt his absence.

Once or twice Paige tried to catch Charles's eye, hoping for some expression of empathy, of understanding or reassurance. But both times his head was inclined either toward Lady Ursula or Demetra, as he listened to whatever they were saying.

Suddenly Paige became aware of a general movement around the table. Charles rose and assisted Lady Ursula from her chair, then came around to Paige.

He smiled, and immediately all her silly imaginings took flight. Of course Charles loved her. Everything would work out. She had only to believe that what she had engraved on the watch fob was true.

The rest of the evening passed pleasantly enough. Demetra brought out a board game that required no verbal skills, just concentration and focus, so that Paige could play too. Of course, she missed some of the usual verbal interaction during any such game. Finally, at ten o'clock, her grandmother rose to say she was retiring. Demetra accompanied her upstairs, and at last Paige had a chance to be alone with Charles.

She went over to him, put her arms around him, and lifted her face for his kiss. But Charles seemed to stiffen. Something was different between them. In times past when they were alone together after a long evening with others, they had both found eager release in expressing their affections. Charles had been an ardent lover and Paige responsive.

A disturbing possibility struck her. Had her deafness become a barrier? Before she could determine if it was only her imagination or something real, Charles gently took her hands from around his neck and led her over to the sofa. Then from his waistcoat he drew out the little notebook he carried now and wrote rapidly. Puzzled, Paige waited until he handed it to her. Her eyes raced across the words he had written. *I'm sorry, I haven't had a chance to tell you. I am being assigned to a limited tour of duty in Ireland. I shall be stationed there for four to six months.*

"Oh no!" Paige gasped. Dismay merged with unreasonable anger and frustration. "Oh, no, you can't go! Please, no. Not now!"

Charles shook his head, reached for the notepad again, and wrote more. *There is new trouble in Ireland. It is hoped the British presence there will be a deterrent to further problems. It's too complicated to explain. You will just have to accept it. Even if we were wed, I would have to go. Orders are orders. I'm a soldier; I obey orders.*

"Oh, no, I can't bear it. First Thatcher, now you!" Unable to control herself, Paige began to sob. She flung herself on Charles, her head on his shoulder. She knew he must be speaking to her, but if the truth be known, she didn't want to hear, knowing his words were surely about being calm and brave. Didn't he realize that brave was the last thing she wanted to be, could be? She wanted to scream, beat her fists against his chest, beg him not to leave her.

He took her chin in his hand, lifted her face, and looked at her. She saw disappointment in his expression. She shut her eyes. She didn't want to see his disappointment. She didn't care if she was behaving badly.

"It's too cruel. If you go, I shall be all alone."

Charles shook his head and took the notepad again. *Nonsense. Not alone at all. Demetra has promised to stay and help out in every possible way.*

Demetra! Paige dismissed the thought and turned away. What possible help could *she* be? Paige felt the old, familiar childhood sense of loneliness and abandonment once again.

*T*hatcher's absence was strongly felt at Mallory Hall; he had always exerted a certain presence. His vitality, his sense of humor, his ability to turn the ordinary into something special was now sadly missing. Lady Ursula, who doted on him, missed him too. He had cajoled her out of her frequent stormy moods and amused her by regaling her with stories of the people at social events that she no longer attended but liked hearing about.

With Thatcher gone and Charles now stationed in Ireland, Paige felt doubly bereft. To assuage some of her loneliness, she began writing long letters to Thatcher, pouring out her heart.

*Dear Thatcher,*

*Since you are not here for me to complain to directly, I shall, as they say in old-fashioned books, take pen in hand and write to you instead.*

*We all miss you terribly. Demetra tries to fill in the gap for Grandmother, reading to her, engaging her in conversation, and playing the piano for her. I should* be grateful, since I cannot do any of those things with her myself.

Great-aunt Enid has left. She thought Mallory Hall drafty and dull and went home to her own fireside and bed. Besides the servants, there are now only the three of us left—Grandmother, Demetra, and me. I am puzzled that Demetra is still here. After my wedding was postponed, there was no reason for her to stay. One day I asked her why she has stayed on, and she wrote, Grandmother has asked me to remain, and my employer, Lady Hadley, has agreed. I thought the rift between Grandmother and her stepdaughter, Demetra's mother, had never been reconciled. Perhaps I am wrong. Do you know?

Time drags dreadfully for me these days. I feel so shut out. This silent world I inhabit is like a kind of solitary confinement. Every sound is silenced—footsteps, voices, doors opening and shutting—I feel so alone.

I think a great deal about our childhood and how it was when I first came to Mallory Hall as a seven-year-old child. Everything seemed so new and strange, so different from what it had been before when I lived at Halcyon Court with my father. Everything at Mallory Hall was so austere, so formal. Ancestral portraits, antiques, parquet floors, polished paneling, Persian rugs. At Halcyon Court everything was worn and comfortable, with the dogs allowed inside and scratches on the floors ignored. At Mallory Hall, when we were old enough to eat in the dining room, the meals were so tedious. Do you remember? Squirming and eager to be off to our own childish pursuits, we had to sit through at least eight courses. At Halcyon Coust, meals were casual and haphazard, a meat pie or roast, garden vegetables piled high on plates, cobblers or pies made of fruit from our orchard. What I missed most when I first came to Mallory Hall was my pony, Princess.

Lest you think I am demoralized and being morbid about the past, I will tell you I do see some progress. I'm gradually regaining my physical strength. Today I walked down to the stables to visit Mayling and also Templar, the mount Charles rode when he was here on weekends. Templar's mane is almost exactly the color of Charles's hair. I think that's one reason I chose Templar for him. It makes me sad not to be able to tell the groom to saddle up Mayling so I can be off for a brisk canter. But Dr. Grantly has forbidden it so far. He says my hearing loss can easily affect my balance, and riding would be dangerous until it is restored. Dangerous! With my sweet mare, who is so easy to manage? I can't help but think of the mornings we rode through the misty meadows with no thought of injury or troubles. I know, I know! I can just hear you say, "Be patient, Mopsy, all that will happen again." But when? I get so impatient, Thatcher. It seems a century since my illness began. How I long to turn the clock back to December, before any of this happened!

I should close lest my melancholy ramblings depress you. Know that you are missed and loved and longed for here.

Always yours, Mopsy

Dear Thatcher,

I have the oddest feeling that when I walk into a room the conversation stops, whether it's Grandmother and Demetra or Dr. Grantly or the housekeeper or Grandmother's lawyer. Are they discussing me? I wonder. If they are, I can't blame them. I'm afraid I have become very hard to get along with since I lost my hearing.

Or have I always been this restless, so easily irritated, so easily offended? I don't think so. The last few times Charles was here, before he went to Ireland, I admit I actually precipitated little quarrels over foolish things. No wonder he found Demetra more pleasant company.

The last person on earth I wanted to alienate was Charles. I worried all the time about losing him, and yet I did things to annoy and aggravate him—perhaps to test him. It is the thought that this deafness may not be temporary, that I will always be deaf, that drove me to it. If it is permanent, how can I live with it? How can Charles live with it? I shall be a hindrance to his career.

Oh, Thatcher, I miss you so. I miss the way we used to talk and pour out our hearts to each other. I wish Charles were as open as you about his feelings. I don't know how he feels about my deafness. Does it frighten him? Repulse him? Embarrass him?

I don't know. I can't tell. How I wish you were here instead of thousands of miles away, across the ocean.

Ever yours, Mopsy

*Dear Thatcher,*

*For all my good intentions, I find myself moping around this large, empty house. I am becoming someone I don't recognize. I know you were right when you told me I was the only one who could find the key to how to live with this—if I must live with it. That's just it, Thatcher. I keep thinking there must be a way, if only I could find it.*

*Every morning I wake up and test myself. And every morning I am crushed with disappointment. No sound—just silence.*

*I cannot accept that I may always live without hearing beautiful music, church bells, the song of the meadowlarks in the early morning when I'm out riding—and will I ever ride again? I get cold with fear at the possibility of a life without all this. And what about Charles? He will have to share this burden with me. It's not what he bargained for when he proposed marriage. I'm afraid I shall lose him. What man would want a wife who cannot participate fully in the things he enjoys? Or even hear them?*

*Always yours, Mopsy*

Paige also wrote long letters to Charles, letters filled with her days' happenings. She described her visits to the stables, good books she had read, and her purchases from mornings spent shopping with Demetra. Somehow, even though she included little endearments and thoughts about their future plans together, the new ache of uncertainty in her heart would not go away. Relief came only in pouring out her thoughts and fears to Thatcher. Relief came, too, in finally receiving and reading Thatcher's replies from India after weeks of waiting.

Charles's letters from Ireland came more swiftly, of course, but they seemed cold and distant somehow. If his military bearing made him seem formal in person, it was all the more accentuated by the distance between them now. She found little that spoke of warm affection or loving reassurance in his terse, neatly penned lines. He strictly avoided mentioning the nature of her illness.

Thatcher never failed to encourage her, though, even in regard to her fears about Charles and their future. He knew how to comfort and confront her and did both, which made her value their unique relationship all the more. Reading and rereading Thatcher's words, she missed him more than ever.

*Dear Mopsy,*

*Our letters must have crossed. I wrote you on board ship, but could not mail letters until our first port of call. I am now in Calcutta and have received your letters. I read them through several times—I must admit with some dismay. You must not lose heart.*

*Self-pity is natural, but only justified if from it comes new resolution to overcome whatever we're facing. Dr. Grantly himself told you this loss of hearing is quite possibly temporary, only a result of your long illness. Your hearing may return at any time. We have always counted on each other for the truth. My affection and concern for you do not change with time and the distance between us.*

*As regards Charles, it may be his military training that has caused his inability to show emotion. A military academy like Sandhurst is not known to turn out overly sensitive poets! If your love is true, deep,* and strong, what you two are going through should strengthen your relationship. The marriage vows promise "in sickness and in health." Surely he can see beyond these temporary difficulties to the woman he fell in love with and proposed to marry. I'll stop all this "sermonizing" for now and get this letter off to you.

Fondly, Thatcher

PS By the way, you asked about Demetra and about Lady Ursula's relationship with Aunt Helena and her husband, Basil Colfax. From what I gather, Demetra contacted your grandmother for a reference when she applied for the job as governess to Lady Imelda Hadley's children. A correspondence then developed between them. I suppose Lady Ursula felt some guilt about cutting Demetra and her mother, Helena, so completely out of her life after Lord Mallory's death. I know Aunt Helena pleaded with her to cover the amount Basil allegedly embezzled from the firm. Lady Ursula could have prevented his going to jail. But she wouldn't. She despised Colfax and wouldn't relent. But now she may feel some sense of obligation to Demetra, especially since Demetra has become so accommodating and useful. However, I do not think her forgiveness extends to Basil. I was only twelve at the time, but I was old enough to realize the seriousness of those terrible events when they took place.

Dear Mopsy,
Three of your letters have just reached me, and although

you will receive my response long after your need for what I have to say, I still hasten to answer them.

I try to understand what you are feeling. I know no one else can fully take on another's pain, the old griefs, the yearning for remembered happiness, but I do want to remind you of something you may have forgotten, overwhelmed as you feel from your loss of hearing—which I repeat, may be temporary.

There is so much more to each of us than physical appearance or faculties. There is heart, soul, and spirit. You are unique, Mopsy, don't you know that? Doesn't Charles see beyond that outer façade of a picture-perfect army officer's wife to the splendid woman you are capable of becoming?

You wrote of remembering our childhood days at Mallory Hall. I can identify well with what it must have been like for you, coming up from the country and your casual existence at Halcyon Court with your father. The sense of loneliness we both shared at Mallory Hall, the loss of loving parents. But I think that loss may have given us some things we still have and must hold on to: strength, faith, confidence. As children we weathered a lot of storms. And we still can. You must be strong, believe, and have confidence in your God-given abilities. Read Joshua 1:9: "Be strong and of good courage; do not be afraid, nor be dismayed, for the LORD your God is with you wherever you go."

Remember, I am counting on you, trusting you to come through this with flying colors.

Ever yours, Thatcher

32

Aside from her father long ago, few people in her life had told Paige she was special. She had often wondered what purpose there could be in losing her parents so early and going to the austere Mallory Hall to live with her reserved grandmother.

She had wondered what purpose there could be for her at all. She had always taken for granted the privileges and comforts of her parents' wealth, but the endless round of social engagements and pleasurable activities had come to an abrupt halt as a result of her illness.

The prospect of marrying a handsome army officer and perhaps traveling with him or raising their children in a home of her own had given Paige something new to look forward to, a new purpose. But her dreams of escaping Mallory Hall by becoming a new bride had also come to an abrupt halt. The sameness of everyday life at Mallory Hall had become even more oppressive since she had been confined by her illness. Her wedding was postponed, and both her hearing and her fiancé were gone, at least for the present.

She had only the possibility, not the promise, that her hearing would return. Yet while she had the promise of Charles's return, it was accompanied by a gnawing fear. She began to fear the possibility that he might not want to come back to her in her current condition.

The events past and present caused both grief and bitterness. Reading Thatcher's letters, though, Paige began to heal and to hope, despite her present physical disability. Could Thatcher be right? Was she becoming a unique, splendid woman? Was she a stronger person as a result of her difficulties, and could anything good come out of them? She knew of one thing she must be thankful for—her course of events had brought her and Thatcher together. He had been like a brother in childhood, a playmate, companion, and best friend. The two of them had been inseparable, and now, though separated from each other, he was still her strongest ally and support. She must write and tell him she would try harder to live up to his words.

Dear Thatcher,

Thank you for your stern but loving reminder of what I should be thankful for, rather than complaining. Perhaps I am romanticizing about the past and not properly appreciating the present or the lessons to be learned. My memories of my mother are vague: an elegant, glamorous, graceful vision, the fragrance of violets, the softness of furs, the glitter of jewels. Father's is a clearer, stronger image. When we lived at Halcyon Court and Mother was off enjoying the London season, I hardly missed her. But you are right. We both must surely be stronger people now, having had to rely on ourselves and each other growing up. I must stop feeling sorry for myself and count my blessings. You are first among them! I shall try harder.

Lovingly, Mopsy

Dear Thatcher,

Perhaps you think I lack sufficient diversion these days, so I while away the hours dreaming up mischief, dwelling on all sorts of suspicions, and feeling sorry for myself. I do try to imagine what kind of good works a deaf lady can do, but I come up woefully short.

By chance (or perhaps I should use the phrase our governess often used—divine coincidence) this morning, however, I saw something in the newspaper. As you know, ladies are not supposed to read the newspaper except for the society pages, the court news, and what the royals are doing. However, I do believe it is significant that I saw this particular item and read it.

It was an announcement of a lecture to be given in London by a noted audiologist (specialist in hearing disorders), Dr. Alistair Sinclair. He will speak about the clinic he heads in Edinburgh, where he teaches a new method of lipreading for the deaf. The date is a week from today! When I read this, I knew at once I must go and find out more. It seems like the light at the end of the tunnel, a possibility to move again in the real world without calling attention to my impairment. Imagine me carrying around some large hearing device (a trumpet!). Perhaps I could follow and participate in conversations by learning how mouth movements shape words. Somehow I knew I must get to the lecture. But how? I could never go alone. I would need someone with me who could hear. That's where another unexpected incident fits in—all being of divine direction.

I knew I needed Grandmother's permission to attend the lecture, so I tore out the announcement and rushed into her sitting room. Demetra was there reading to her. I handed Grandmother the article about Alistair Sinclair and his simplified way for the deaf to communicate using both lipreading and sign language.

When I showed Grandmother the clipping, her first reaction was negative. She frowned and wrote to me: What good would it do you to attend the lecture? You could not hear what he said.

I glanced at Demetra. "Demetra could go with me and take notes. The main thing is that I could meet him myself and explain my situation. This article says he has a clinic in Scotland where he holds seminars especially for the deaf. Perhaps it would be possible for me to go."

At this Grandmother looked shocked and wrote: To Scotland?

It was then that I said what is in my heart and what I'd never said to anyone but you before. "I cannot go on living in this half-world. To be shut off from everything I love—everyone I care about, especially Charles. Don't you see that?" I asked her.

I could go on to tell you about Grandmother's many objections and my answers, but then Demetra surprised us both by telling Grandmother she would accompany me to the lecture. Grandmother finally agreed to let her do so. If, after hearing Dr. Sinclair, I still want to attend his institute in Scotland, she will decide then. Her final word was: I shall have to consult Dr. Grantly and have him check on the background of this man. He could be a charlatan, you know, preying on desperate people.

I do not believe it. His work has given me some hope.

Lovingly, Mopsy

4

*T*he day of Dr. Sinclair's lecture was overcast. Gray skies threatened rain, and as midafternoon approached, it began to drizzle. Paige worried that, considering her recent illness, this might give Grandmother reason to protest her going out.

Demetra's reassurance successfully overruled Grandmother's last-minute objections. Since Thompson, the coachman, would leave them off in front of the building and be there to pick them up when the lecture was over, there was no chance of them getting chilled or wet.

By the time they reached London, it was raining hard. Early evening traffic was heavy, and carriages, cabs, and coaches of all sizes, with their occupants on their way to theaters, dinners, and parties, crowded the streets and tangled with carts and wagons. The hall where Dr. Sinclair was scheduled to speak was in an unfashionable part of the city. Thompson, unfamiliar with this part of London, had to stop twice to ask for directions. As the scheduled time for the lecture neared, Paige began to feel tense. When they at last found their way to the right street, it was raining harder than ever. Upon seeing the crush of vehicles dispersing passengers in front, Paige tugged at Demetra's arm and insisted they get out and walk the short distance to the hall. After jumping puddles and desperately holding on to their umbrellas, they hurried up the steps. Inside, they shed their capes and shook their umbrellas.

They bought their tickets, gave them to an usher, and were shown to seats quite close to the stage. As they settled into their seats, a man stepped up to the podium and began addressing the audience in sign language.

"Demetra," Paige whispered urgently, "your notebook. You didn't forget it, did you?"

Demetra shook her head and drew a small notebook and pencil from her muff. Paige sat on the edge of her seat, breathing shallowly, waiting for the arrival of Alistair Sinclair.

At length, a tall, rather stoop-shouldered man walked onto the stage and over to the lectern, where he put on wire-rimmed glasses and assembled his notes. Then he began to speak. A woman in the background interpreted his words in sign language.

Since Paige could not hear his words, she closely observed his face. She also often glanced at Demetra to make sure she was paying attention and jotting down notes.

At last the lecture drew to a close. Alistair Sinclair looked at the man and woman who had been signing and said something to them, which they immediately signed to the audience.

"What's going on?" Paige asked Demetra.

She wrote, *He said he'd be glad to answer any questions.*

Paige had some questions to ask. Most important to her was whether she had any chance of recovering her hearing. If so, what would be best for her to do? And if not, how could she best move back into the world she had planned with Charles, a world where she must be able to socialize and communicate without being conspicuous?

Paige clutched Demetra's arm. "I *must* speak to him. Can we go backstage? Or make an appointment to see him privately?"

Demetra looked doubtful.

"Please, Demetra, I have to." Paige's voice was not only insistent, it must also have been loud, since Demetra darted a rather embarrassed look over both shoulders. But Paige was already on her feet. A woman behind them tapped Demetra's arm and said something to her. Demetra wrote to Paige: *He has a handbook, an instructional manual in signing. He'll be selling and autographing them in the lobby. Follow me.*

When Paige and Demetra reached the back of the hall, a line was already queued up in front of Alistair Sinclair. He sat at a table piled high with handbooks, and as he autographed each one, he took a few minutes to talk to the individual. He seemed unhurried and very kind. The line moved slowly on that account. Demetra pressed Paige's arm and held up her notebook: *Wait here. I'll go see if Thompson is out front. In this crowd he may not be able to hold his place.*

Only three people stood in front of Paige now. Then at last it was her turn. Where was Demetra? Paige stepped forward alone. She handed Sinclair a handbook to sign and immediately began to tell him her situation.

He halted writing and looked up at her. Behind his spectacles his eyes regarded her intently. Paige felt he understood her desperation. He scribbled a note and held it up for her to read. *How long have you been without your hearing?*

She told him, and he nodded again and wrote very fast: *I think we can help you at the clinic. I am partially deaf myself, an injury in childhood. One ear is worse than the other, but I can hear and understand you. I can also read lips, so you don't have to raise your voice.*

Paige felt her face flush; she hadn't realized she was talking so loudly. Alistair Sinclair was writing something more: *Since you lost your hearing so recently, I suggest you learn lipreading as a better way to communicate.* He tapped his handbook with a forefinger. *All the information about my training courses is in here. Contact me if you're interested in coming to my institute in Scotland.*

His assistant handed Paige a printed slip of paper. *Your questions are answered in this booklet. You can write directly to the institute for any further information.*

Paige felt movement behind her and knew the people in line were growing restless; she had already taken up extra time. She took the booklet and thanked Dr. Sinclair. Turning around to look for Demetra, Paige didn't see her at first. Then she spotted her standing at the entrance, deep in conversation with a man in a dark cape. His back was to Paige, so she couldn't see his face. At first she thought it was Thompson, then she wasn't so sure. As she watched, the man hurried off down the steps into the rainy night. For a minute Demetra stood looking after him, then slowly turned and walked back toward Paige.

She seemed preoccupied as she wrote on her pad: *Hurry, we must go. It's chaos out there. Carriages are lined up behind Thompson. It is such a miserable night, people are getting annoyed at being kept waiting.* Then she took Paige's arm.

Paige could sense the impatience and tension in her cousin. Demetra kept a tight hold on Paige's arm and hurried her out into the chill night. As they stood shivering on the steps and looking for the Mallory coach, Paige was surprised to see a man standing at the horses' heads by the harness lead as Thompson maneuvered the carriage closer. She thought it odd that a stranger would offer such assistance. On second glance, she saw he was the same man to whom Demetra had been talking. He was wearing the same type cape and slouch hat. Is that what they had been discussing? Had Demetra arranged for him to lead Thompson out of the melee so it would be easier to get into the carriage? Were there men who frequented London's public places like theaters and lecture halls and offered such services?

Demetra held on to Paige as they made their way through the crowd and down the steps. The man tipped his wide-brimmed hat dripping with rain and opened the carriage door for them. Demetra touched Paige's purse, indicating she should give him something for his trouble. Paige had no idea how much.

Demetra reached for Paige's purse and took out a sovereign. She placed it in the man's outstretched palm, and the two women got into the carriage.

Brimming over with enthusiasm about Alistair Sinclair and the encouragement he had given her, Paige chattered as they wove their way out of the traffic and turned onto the road leading back to Mallory Hall.

"I'm sure Grandmother will agree to allowing me to go to Dr. Sinclair's clinic in Scotland when I explain it all and she reads the handbook. Don't you think so, Demetra? And I can't wait to tell Charles. I have been so worried about him. I am afraid he thinks I am a hopeless case. I haven't been myself, that's for certain. It's only because I didn't want to be a burden or an embarrassment to him, but now I can see a way of getting my life back. Dr. Sinclair says his system is easier for people who already have their speech pattern and have *heard* other people talk. It is a familiarity with intonations, rises and falls, and the subtle things people who hear never even think about that makes such a difference in cultivating normal speech once you have lost your hearing." Paige gave a happy little bounce on the seat and clapped her hands. "Oh, Demetra, for the first time in ages I feel really optimistic about the future. If I can only get Grandmother to agree."

It was dark inside the carriage, and the rain-shrouded night made it impossible to see Demetra's reaction.

Paige wasted no time. The very next day she filled out the application to the Sinclair Institute and sent it off. Of course, she knew persuading Lady Ursula to let her go to Scotland for the six weeks of training was a huge hurdle she must vault even if she was accepted in the class. In her next letter to Thatcher she described the whole situation.

Dear Thatcher,

I am writing this in such excitement I hardly know how to tell you. So much has happened so quickly. I am about to embark on a venture that has indeed given me new hope. I know you have been concerned about my state of mind. But all that is completely changed now.

In a few days I am leaving for Scotland, because I am enrolled in Alistair Sinclair's clinic for the deaf. I sent you his brochure outlining his method for teaching the hearing-impaired to communicate in various ways. The most common and easiest to learn is sign language. The newer form is lipreading, which I want to try. This way no one else is involved, just the deaf person. This would be less noticeable and simpler to integrate into social situations with hearing people, which, of course, is most important for me. I would not want Charles to be embarrassed by me, nor do I want to make myself an object of pity.

Just as you predicted, things are working out for me, or as our former governess would quote from the Bible, "All things work together for good to those who love God, to those who are the called according to His purpose." I'm not sure that I exactly fit into that description. I know my purpose is rather selfish. I want to be the best possible wife for Charles and not deter his advancement in his army career.

The training seems intense and severe. The student remains incommunicado with the outside world while at the institute. It is learning by immersion, as they call it. I am sure it will be worth it. At least I will be with other similarly afflicted people, and we will be able to practice communicating with each other before we return to the ordinary hearing world.

I know you will rejoice with me over this turn of events. It is like seeing the proverbial light at the end of the tunnel, which this deafness has seemed to be to me.

Let me give you a thumbnail sketch of what led up to all this. After I attended Sinclair's lecture, I knew I had to go to the clinic. But since I am underage, I first needed to get Grandmother's permission.

Picture Grandmother's sitting room, me eager and anxiously hoping to win her case, Grandmother writing furiously on her notepad: Scotland at this time of year? It will be cold and damp. What do we know about the accommodations at this clinic? You were very much weakened by your illness. I believe it would be a grave risk to your health to make the trip north into so uncertain a situation.

"But, Grandmother, I am fully recovered physically— even Dr. Grantly will confirm that."

Grandmother wrote: There is no guarantee that this will do you any good.

I was desperate and tried pleading. "I know it is an experiment, but it is worth the risk. If I don't try this, I shall be truly despondent. Please say you'll agree."

It was at this point that I received the most unexpected support. Demetra, who had been observing all of this, spoke up. Of course, I couldn't hear anything she was saying, but whatever she said worked. Grandmother gave in and granted permission for me to go to Scotland for training at the Sinclair Institute. I was amazed that Demetra would come to my aid! The night of the lecture she had seemed distracted, indifferent, even bored.

Thatcher, I must tell you what I believe closed the argument for Grandmother. When she hesitated to give me permission, I played a card I have never used with her before. I said as calmly as I could manage, "I can go now, Grandmother, with your permission, or I can wait until next October when I am twenty-one and in charge of my own money and my own decisions."

Maybe that was unkind of me to remind her of my inheritance, but Thatcher, I am willing to risk everything to have the chance to communicate again.

This has been all about me, I realize, but I assure you that you have been in my thoughts and prayers every day since you left. I have missed you dreadfully, our long talks, your constant support and encouragement. We will have so much to talk about and tell each other when you return. And then we won't have to use paper and pen to communicate. I should be an expert in lipreading by that time. Everything is going ahead. We sent all the necessary papers, Dr. Grantly's report on my health (necessary but reluctantly given, I must add), and a cheque to enroll me in the course. Demetra is making the travel arrangements. She will accompany me to London, where I will take the train to Edinburgh. There someone from the Sinclair Institute will meet me.

With fondest love, always yours, Mopsy

he night before Paige was to leave for Scotland, she moved back and forth between her trunk and suitcase, evaluating their contents. Her grandmother was right. It would be cold and rainy in Scotland at this time of year, so Flora had packed plenty of warm things—sweaters, jackets, flannel underwear.

As she checked her dressing-table drawers, she saw the small velvet box containing her engagement ring. The doctor had removed it when she became ill, and she had not worn it since because she had lost so much weight that it was too big for her finger. Paige opened the lid, removed the ring, and slipped it on. It was still too big. Truthfully, she had never liked the ring—a large ruby in a heavy, ornate setting. Charles told her it had belonged to his mother, which she supposed should make her feel honored. But it didn't suit her, and she thought it rather ugly. She would have preferred a smaller ring, maybe an opal, her birthstone, one that Charles chose himself and could reasonably afford on his lieutenant's pay. She placed the ring in the box now. It was probably too valuable to risk wearing to Scotland and possibly losing.

The next morning Flora bade Paige a teary good-bye and carried her bags downstairs to where Grandmother and Demetra already stood in the front hall. Lady Ursula had numerous parting instructions. These, however, were directed to Demetra. She handed Demetra several envelopes—one containing a letter of credit to use, the second the remainder of Paige's tuition for the course, the third money for train fare and travel expenses.

Paige bit back an indignant protest that surely she could handle these things herself. Since she'd become deaf, her grandmother often acted as if she'd lost her mind as well as her hearing. Anyway, she had her own money. Ever since her boarding school days, she had received a monthly allowance from her trust fund. Besides, she was too happy, too excited to take much offense at anything. Not wanting any friction at leaving, she simply kissed her grandmother, said good-bye, and went out to the waiting carriage. She was off on a great adventure, one she hoped and prayed would bring her back into the world she'd lost.

Early morning London was cloaked in fog but alive with people ready to start their workaday lives. Carriages and omnibuses, lorries and drays jammed the thoroughfare. Wagon drivers waved their arms and shouted at each other. Ragged newsboys and street peddlers were already out and about their business.

Paige was on the edge of her seat as they moved through the city. Once they arrived at the railroad station, Thompson unloaded Paige's belongings, and Demetra motioned for him to find a place to park the carriage.

The platform was crowded with passengers with their luggage piled high around them. Demetra frowned, then took a few steps forward waving her hand, obviously trying to hail a porter. At last one pulling a cart stopped, and Demetra pointed to Paige's trunk, valise, and tea basket. He shoved them onto his already half-full cart and started trundling them away. Demetra motioned to Paige to follow. They had to hurry to keep up with him as he darted ahead, dodging haphazardly around groups of travelers on the platform. He was already loading her belongings into one of the first-class compartments when they caught up with him. Demetra gave him a generous tip, then pulled out her notepad and wrote: *I'm going back to the newsstand to get you a box of chocolates and a magazine to read on the train.*

A woman standing nearby glanced at them curiously, a countrywoman by the look of her, in an old-fashioned poke bonnet and a voluminous plaid shawl.

"You don't need to do that," Paige said a little sharply to Demetra as she moved past the woman onto the train and into the compartment. But Demetra went off and was soon lost in the crowd.

Paige felt guilty that she had been short with Demetra. It was kind of her to offer something to read and chocolates to eat on the way. However, Paige really didn't need anything. In fact, she could have managed without Demetra coming with her to see her off. Thompson could have escorted her to the Highland Express and seen her settled into her compartment. When the train reached Edinburgh, someone from the Sinclair Institute would be there to meet her.

Paige checked her pendant watch and saw that it was almost time for the train to leave. She looked out the compartment window and saw the conductor coming down the platform, slamming each door shut. That meant imminent departure. She watched as other passengers said their farewells and started to board the train. Suddenly Paige became tense.

Where was Demetra? She looked in the direction in which she had disappeared and began to feel nervous. If Demetra didn't hurry, the train would leave. Then, in a moment of horror, Paige realized Demetra had the ticket! What would she do if Demetra didn't return with it in time? She supposed she could buy another from the conductor after the train started, but, oh, Demetra had most of the money as well. Paige got up and stepped out of the compartment onto the platform, desperately looking for her cousin. Demetra was nowhere in sight among the people rushing down the platform, jostling each other.

Suddenly Paige forgot about Demetra when the country-woman who had been watching them earlier gripped her arm and held on tight. Startled, Paige tried to pull away, but the woman's grip was strong, and Paige had never fully re-gained her strength since her illness. The woman propelled Paige through the crowd. The more Paige struggled to break free, the more painfully the woman squeezed her arm.

"Stop, let me go!" Paige gasped, but the woman did not slow her step nor loosen her viselike grip—it only tightened. They were back inside the station now, and the woman was walking faster and faster, almost dragging Paige along. Paige glanced around frantically for Demetra. What was this all about? Panicked, Paige tried to scream. Was this woman going to rob her? Paige's throat felt constricted, her breathing choked. Her eyes moved from person to person as they passed each one. Couldn't they see what was happening? But no one seemed to notice. Everyone looked straight ahead, rushing forward, intent only on their own purposes. Then, with a final tug, the woman pulled Paige through the station door into the cold morning. Paige was aware of the acrid smell of coal cinders combined with the smells of the city. The fog was still thick and whirling about, blurring the fig-ures entering the terminal. The woman yanked Paige roughly, and suddenly, with a final thrust, shoved her into a dark alleyway.

A man appeared out of nowhere as if he had been wait-ing for them. Extreme panic washed over Paige now. She couldn't cry out but just thought *God help me!* The man took her by the shoulders and twisted her arms behind her back, while the woman threw her huge shawl over Paige, covering her head and face. Paige felt her wrists being bound tightly with a rough rope.

Wedged in by the two bodies pressed on either side of her, Paige was dragged a little farther, her screams muffled by the heavy shawl. Still held securely, she was pushed inside something, a sort of wagon with doors. There the shawl was whipped off, and for the first time she saw the man as he thrust his face close to hers. Ugly features contorted into a kind of grimace revealing blackened, rotten teeth. He snarled something she knew was threatening. She opened her mouth to scream, and he roughly pushed her head down and thrust a filthy rag in her mouth, securing the rag with a tight knot.

Paige shrank back, her body trembling. The doors slammed. She felt the shake of the lock as it bolted the doors, leaving her in the musty dark. A few minutes later she felt a jolting lurch as the vehicle moved forward. She fell back on her elbows. Where were they taking her? The roughness of the ride revealed they were on cobblestones. She moved across the floor as best she could and kicked against the doors, but it was no use. Screams rose in her throat again, but the gag muffled her cries, as did the sound of the wheels and the horses' hooves. How could anyone possibly hear her?

Weak and sick with fear, she leaned against the side of the wagon. Her head pounded, as did her heart. Her shoulders and arms ached from the rough way the two had handled her. Her wrists stung where they had been chafed in her efforts to twist them free of their bonds. Her breathing was shallow; she was so frightened it was impossible to draw a full breath. The cloth jammed into her mouth made breathing even more difficult.

City crooks were sly and cunning. They planted themselves in places like railroad stations, where people were distracted and careless and flashed money without thinking. Anyone could easily watch the travelers with evil intent. Still, if these two had just wanted her money, the woman could easily have snatched her purse and gotten away before Demetra returned. So why hadn't she?

Paige knew her handbag only contained a few sovereigns, a handkerchief, some lip balm, and a small bottle of scent. Demetra had most of the money. Had they mistaken her for Demetra? If anyone was watching, looking for rich victims, they would have seen Demetra tip the porter.

Who were these terrible people? And why had they abducted her? What was their evil intent?

After what seemed an agonizingly long time, the wagon came to a stop. A minute later the doors were flung open. Paige tensed for whatever might come next.

She had completely lost track of time. She had no idea how long or how far they had traveled from the railroad station. It was dark, and someone was holding a lantern. A man's bulky figure blocked the light. He glared at her, but Paige did not move. Then he reached in and grabbed her arm roughly, pulling her forward. She tried to shake off his hand, but he only tightened his grip. She felt his hot breath tinged with the odor of whiskey on her face as he yanked her into a sitting position, then dragged her down out of the wagon.

He turned to the woman behind him, and in the light shed on her face Paige saw her unpleasant expression. Deep lines made grooves on either side of her mouth, and her eyes were narrowed into slits. She moved around to the other side of Paige and took her upper arm, her stubby fingers pressing through the material of Paige's coat.

"Let go of me!" Paige shouted through the gag.

They paid no attention and together bundled her along a rutted path and up some steps into a dimly lit house.

They were both breathing hard from pulling Paige, who continued to resist. They dragged her up some more wooden steps and into a narrow hall. Inside, the man took off his cap and wiped his forehead with the back of his arm. The woman, red faced and puffing, leaned against the wall.

At last Paige could take a good look at both of them. The man was large and barrel chested and was wearing workmen's clothes. He stared at her with hooded eyes in a pudgy face. Paige recoiled from the presence of evil she felt from him.

He said something to the woman, who then took hold of Paige's arm and began to pull her along the shadowy hallway. Paige struggled all the way, making it as hard as she could for the woman. However, the woman was strong, and Paige knew her fear was weakening her resistance. Where were they taking her? What were they going to do to her?

At the end of the hall the woman used her other arm to open a door. She thrust Paige inside and slammed the door.

Paige was in total darkness. She slumped against the wall. Her wrists were rubbed raw in her attempts to free them from the coarse rope. Her throat hurt, parched by her useless screams. Gradually her eyes became used to the darkness, and she glanced around. It was some kind of a storage room, empty except for a few sticks of furniture. Where had they brought her? It must be outside London. The trip had seemed so long. That terrible man and his female accomplice were surely criminals of some kind. Was this planned? Or had they just picked a random victim? Were they part of a gang? Could this really be a kidnapping? With a shudder, Paige recalled the stories she'd heard of young women captured and sold into a kind of slavery beyond imagination.

And what about Demetra? What had she done when she found Paige gone? When the train left? Did she go to the police and tell them her deaf cousin was missing? Surely someone saw Paige being dragged away by that woman, visibly protesting, struggling. Or was everyone so self-absorbed they hadn't noticed? Paige tried to remember what had actually happened, but it had all happened so fast it now seemed unreal. Everything blurred. Her vivid imagination conjured up all sorts of horrible possibilities. She'd read and heard about assaults, robberies, and abductions in sensational newspaper accounts and the awful "shilling" books the housemaids read. But in broad daylight? In a public place? And such heinous acts never happened to people of her social status, *did* they?

The oppressive darkness and her hearing loss increased her feeling of panic. Paige clenched her jaw and determined not to give way to fear. Surely Demetra had gone to the police by now. Even now they could be searching for her. But how would they ever find her? What clues would they have? In the crowded city no one would notice if someone was rushed along attended by a matronly woman. If anyone took notice, they might make the mistake of thinking the victim was having a fit of some kind and was being taken perhaps to the lunatic asylum.

Paige tried to ease the coarse rope against her wrists. Her hat had been knocked off when she was thrown into the wagon, and her hairpins had come loose. Her cheek felt bruised and swollen from hitting the hard floor of the vehicle.

Hours seemed to go by before the door finally opened and the woman entered, holding up a flickering oil lamp. She set down the lamp and bent over Paige. She took out a knife to cut the rope from around her wrists. She pushed Paige's head forward and removed the gag. When it was out of her mouth, Paige coughed and tried to wet her parched lips with her tongue.

The woman's face was so close that Paige could smell her breath, rank with onions and beer. Her ugly mouth moved rapidly. Paige swallowed over her dry throat, and with as much defiance as she could muster, demanded, "Who are you? How dare you bring me here like this? Do you know the penalties for kidnapping?"

The woman spat as she let out a diatribe of some kind. Paige could not hear the words, but she clearly sensed their viciousness.

She struggled to her feet, and although she was taller, the other woman was stout and strong. She grabbed Paige by her upper arm and pulled her out the door and down the hall. At the end, another door stood open. She gave her a hard shove, and Paige felt the resounding vibration as the door slammed shut behind her.

She found herself standing at the top of a flight of narrow wooden steps leading down into what looked like a cellar with small slits of windows along the ceiling. A few candle stubs placed on the windowsills gave off a flickering light. They were the only illumination.

Paige's knees felt wobbly, and she looked for a railing to grab hold of, but there was none. She stood there for a moment trying to get her balance. Then four pale faces appeared at the foot of the steps, all looking up at her.

*O*ne of the figures, a small, skinny girl, moved to the bottom of the stairs. With a hesitant smile she held out her hand as if to help Paige down.

Tentatively, Paige took one step down. She felt shaky, and without a banister it was hard to navigate the narrow boards of the steps. Before she reached the bottom step she tripped, tumbling down the remaining steps and landing with one foot twisted painfully under her.

As she tried to get up, Paige felt two pairs of hands help her to her feet. A sharp pain zigzagged up her leg. Gingerly, she tested her weight on it and winced. She must have sprained her ankle.

The thin girl helping her said something. Paige could tell by the expression on her face that the words were sympathetic. The girl slipped her arm around Paige's waist and helped her sit down on the bottom step.

While Paige looked around, trying to ascertain where they were confined, the girl moved across the room to the window. She walked with a definite limp, dragging one foot. After a moment, she returned carrying a stub of a candle on a cracked saucer, then she took a small box of matches out of her apron pocket and lit the candle. The wavering light gave Paige her first chance to more clearly see the four people who now circled her. Two girls and two boys. They were all so small and scrawny that she couldn't be sure how old they were, but they looked to be between the ages of ten and fifteen. They looked undernourished, shabbily dressed, and disheveled. They all were facing her. Nobody spoke, nobody smiled. Then she noticed one boy's eyes had a murky, glassy look. Was he blind? The other boy's eyes were partially closed, and his face was twisted in a perpetual squint.

Her heart was touched with pity. Who were these poor, neglected youngsters? Why were they here, and what was *she* doing here with them?

The girl who had helped her drew closer, and if her small face, illuminated by the low flame of the dripping candle, had not been grimy with soot, it might have been pretty. The matted hair, too, if it were clean and brushed, might be shiny blond. The girl spoke again.

Paige shook her head and placed both hands over her ears. "I'm deaf. I can't hear what you're saying."

A look of compassion crossed the girl's face. She nodded as if she understood. She held the candle out to Paige.

"Thank you," Paige said, taking it and holding it higher so as to get an idea of where she was. The room was hardly more than a cellar. Mats were spread out on the floor, and a wooden hutch sat in one corner, with a pitcher and bowl on top of it. Two chairs with broken rungs were pushed up against one wall.

The girl held up one hand and hurried over to one of the mats to unroll the blanket. Then she hobbled back with a broken slate and a small piece of chalk in one hand. The other girl, who looked younger and who until now had stood watching, crept up to join them. The older girl then wrote on the slate: *I'm Alice, and this is Mary. She's deaf too. Can you sign? Mary can, and she taught me how.*

Paige shook her head. She started to tell Alice the circumstances of her abduction, that she had been on her way to learn lipreading, but then she stopped. What was the use? It was all so impossible. Why was she trying to explain her terrible circumstances to these poor little girls who were so much worse off than she herself was?

Alice was writing again. *We can teach you signing, then the three of us can be*—she halted, then wrote, *friends.*

Paige felt her heart sink. This wretched little waif was resigned to her lot, as was the other girl. Somehow they expected Paige to do the same—to resign herself to staying here and to learn how to sign so she could communicate with her fellow prisoners. Paige felt on the verge of hysteria as she suddenly realized all of them, herself included, were disabled in some way. The two boys were blind, Alice was crippled, and the other girl, Mary, was deaf.

Paige found herself speechless with rage and despair. How did this happen? What was this place?

Alice looked eager as she waited for Paige's response to her suggestion. Mary also smiled and clapped her hands.

It was too much. Paige knew if she didn't control herself she would burst out crying or laugh maniacally. Instead, she looked around in dismay. "Is this where we're expected to sleep?"

Alice helped Paige to her feet then led her over to the one remaining pallet and pointed to a blanket rolled up on the thin mat.

Fighting tears of outrage, Paige sighed. "I'm very tired."

Alice nodded. She took Mary by the hand and the two turned away and crawled onto their own mats nearby. The others were settling, too, pulling the ragged covers up around them. The candles blew out one by one and Paige was left in the darkness.

There was no use trying to sleep. Her mind was in too much turmoil. She was shivering as much from shock as from the damp cold of this cellar room. Her captors had taken her fur-trimmed coat. She didn't know what had happened to her muff and gloves.

Paige pulled the thin blanket around her shoulders and huddled under its ragged edges. This had to be the worst night of her life. She still hadn't grown used to how frightening darkness is for the deaf. Much worse than for someone who could hear and identify sounds. The imagination creates strange, ominous possibilities lurking in the dark. Paige's imagination had always been her escape, and now it was her enemy. She had never been so wretchedly miserable. Tears rolled down her face unchecked. She buried her head in her hands, quietly sobbing, knowing nobody outside this cellar heard, nobody knew, nobody cared. Tears spent, in spite of her distress and discomfort, she finally drifted off to sleep.

*S*omething awakened Paige. With a jerk she sat up straight, dragged out of the shallow sleep into which she must have fallen. She looked around and shivered as a sick feeling swept over her. It wasn't a nightmare, after all. This was real. She had been kidnapped by unknown persons and brought to this cellar.

Just then, the door at the top of the stairs opened, and the same woman who had dragged her through the railroad station the previous night clumped down. She had shed her mantle of respectability. The bonnet and shawl of yesterday that had caused Paige to peg her as a harmless country-woman were gone. Today she wore a drab dress covered with a checkered apron, and she had a dingy, muslin mobcap on her head.

Paige watched as the woman moved around the cellar room, yanking off blankets, roughly shaking shoulders, rousing the other inmates. Paige was determined to defy her in every way possible if the woman approached her.

The others got up with varying degrees of slowness. Paige felt a stab of compassion. They were hardly more than children, yet they wore the expressions of old people without hope for the future. How had they come to be here? That was a question to which she meant to get an answer. The others stumbled up, folding their blankets, while the woman, hands on her hips, stood glowering. She must have given an order, for now they straggled into a line. She pointed her finger to the stairway, and they shuffled forward. Then she turned her ugly face in Paige's direction and began talking.

Paige deliberately turned her head away, which obviously infuriated the woman. Immediately she was at Paige's side, gripping her arm, but Paige shook her off. Her arms were stiff, and they ached from the rough treatment of the day before; the pain of the woman's touch was excruciating. She grabbed Paige and pulled her halfway up, but Paige resisted. Her twisted foot had swollen during the night and, unable to bear the weight, she refused to stand.

"Don't you dare touch me!" Paige yelled.

The words were hardly out before the woman gave her a slap on the cheek, then pushed her so that she fell back on the pallet. The woman turned to the others, who stood watching, and said something to them.

Alice's eyes grew wide, her expression registering fear at the woman's words. The woman gave Alice a hard shove toward the stairway, then she turned and shook her fist at Paige and followed the others up the stairs.

Paige was left alone in the dark, dank cellar.

She rubbed her cheek, which was still stinging from the slap. She promised herself she would make the woman sorry she had done that. Sorry, too, for all Paige had suffered so far, as well as for the way the woman treated the others who were caught in this same trap.

Beyond Paige's anger and frustration, her physical discomfort was acute. Her stomach was empty and her head ached. She longed for a strong, hot cup of tea to clear her brain, so she could try to puzzle out what to do.

Surely Demetra had reported her missing by now. And had her grandmother been told? Had the police started an investigation? Had Charles been notified? Maybe in this personal crisis, he could get leave. After all, she was his future bride. Surely his commanding officer would bend military rules in such a case.

And Thatcher! Ironically she remembered the letter she had just written him, filled with enthusiasm about going to Alistair Sinclair's clinic in Scotland and her high hopes for the experience. Paige had enclosed one of the handbooks illustrating sign language and outlining the newer method of teaching the deaf to lip-read. If he had received and read her letter, he would think she was well and happy. Paige moaned, "Oh, Thatcher, if you only knew what I am enduring."

Thoughts of Thatcher and all they had shared together came flooding into her mind. Early morning horseback rides through mist-shrouded meadows, the joyous reunions when he came home on school holidays, the pranks and teasing, the quarrels and the laughter, the whispered secrets and shouted disagreements, the competitive games of backgammon and badminton. He'd taught her how to waltz and how to fish. If only he were with her now!

She stirred on the lumpy mat, then shuddered. What was the point in daydreaming now? The dream was gone, leaving her with stark reality. No, this was no time for daydreams. What she needed to do was to think of some way of escape.

*H*ours went by; Paige couldn't tell how many. The couple had taken her small pendant, watch, and her coat and handbag. She had no idea what time it was. The day seemed endless, and her inability to hear anything made it seem longer. She decided to test her sore foot, so she walked carefully across to the slits of windows, where she tried to peer out. They were too high. She then went over to the rickety stairway and, half-crawling, climbed up the steps. Upon reaching the top, she banged her fists on the door—but with no result. Finally she went back down and curled up on the pallet, alternately weeping and praying. "God, please help me. Get me out of here."

Much later, the door at the top of the steps opened, and her four fellow captives returned. They all looked wearier, grimier, and, if possible, older than when the woman had herded them out of the cellar that morning.

Alice glanced at Paige sympathetically. She went to her own mat, then crossed over to Paige's. She carried the slate and a bit of chalk in her hand. On it she wrote: *I'm sorry you were alone all day.* Then she pulled a placard made of cardboard on a yarn string from the pocket of her baggy, knitted sweater and showed it to Paige. Printed in block letters it read: *Please Help Me. I'm A Cripple.* Then she wrote on the slate: *The Brimleys make us go out on the streets every day and beg. Mary has one that says I'm Deaf.*

"That's monstrous!" Paige gasped. "I'll never do that."

Alice wrote: *They'll make you go too.*

"Never!" Paige declared. "I won't!"

Alice shook her head, then underlined the words, *They'll make you.*

"How can they?"

Alice scribbled: *By starving you.*

Paige was already feeling the pangs of hunger. How long could she hold out against such a threat?

The cellar door opened and the jailer, as Paige thought of the woman, stood shining an oil lamp down on them.

Alice ducked behind Paige. She quickly wrote on the slate in big letters, *SUPPER,* then *Her name is Nettie.* She scurried back to her mat, where she hid the slate. She motioned Paige to join the line heading back upstairs.

Paige wanted to resist. Could she be as courageous as those political prisoners she had read about who had gone on hunger strikes? But she knew she needed food to give her strength. She also needed to know the layout of the house. If she refused to leave the cellar, she would never find out where possible exits might be, doors or windows from which she could escape. And Paige had every intention of escaping.

Nettie stood and watched as they came up and marched down the hall. A door stood open leading into a big kitchen. A long table with straight chairs stood in the middle of the room, and a huge, black stove stood at the other end.

Nettie took hold of Paige, jerked her around to one side of the table, and pushed her down into one of the chairs. The other four seated themselves on the other side of the table.

A bowl of some kind of soup was banged down in front of Paige, and a spoon was tossed to one side. Nettie must have given some kind of order, because the four others jumped and immediately picked up their spoons and began to eat.

In the bowl were a few chunks of potatoes and some wilted cabbage leaves floating in a greasy broth. Paige's stomach lurched, but she lifted her spoon and tentatively took a sip. It was unpalatable. Rage overcame caution. She flung down her spoon and pushed back from the table, then whirled around and confronted Nettie. "You expect us to eat this rubbish? What do you think you are doing? You think you can get away with this? I suspect you have kidnapped these children as well. I warn you to release me at once or you will face criminal charges. I will see to it you pay dearly for what you have done to me—"

Nettie looked shocked, then snarled something that Paige was grateful she could not hear. Nettie came toward her with a raised wooden spoon in her hand. In spite of her trembling Paige stood her ground, aware of the four awed spectators across the table. It was probably the first act of defiance they had seen.

Nettie yanked the chair out of the way and grabbed one of Paige's arms so cruelly that Paige let out an involuntary moan. Nettie shouted something at the others, and they all stumbled to their feet. She shoved Paige into the end of the line that quickly formed. She then marshaled them single file back down the corridor, where she yanked open the cellar door and slammed it heavily behind them. As the last one through the door, Paige was pushed and nearly fell on top of the blind boys.

The other four moved slowly down the steps without the benefit of a lamp. For the boys, the lack of light wasn't a problem. Alice, with Mary clinging to her, made it down step by step. Paige waited at the top of the stairway until she became accustomed to the dark.

She was consumed with guilt. Her angering Nettie about the soup had cheated the others out of finishing their supper. Meager as it was, it was all they'd had to eat since morning.

Maybe this was *her* battle alone. Obviously, the others were not capable of putting up a fight. Cowed and intimidated by the two bullies, these children had become so victimized they couldn't fight for themselves. How long had they been here? Was this some kind of institution for the disabled? As soon as Paige asked herself that question, the terrible thought struck. She would be considered disabled too. Questions without answers marched through her mind.

Who had masterminded this? Who knew she was deaf? And how had it been maneuvered? Did they know her grandmother was Lady Ursula Mallory and was thought to be wealthy? They couldn't know that all the Mallory wealth was Paige's. Lady Ursula could not pay a ransom without Paige's countersigning the cheque. It was a monthly ritual Paige dreaded because Lady Ursula so obviously resented it. She hated being dependent on the fortune left by a daughter-in-law she had always detested. Yet that was the way Paige's parents' wills had been drawn up. She was the sole heir, and when she was twenty-one she would inherit the entire estate.

The following evening when they went up to supper, Paige found that her portion was half of what the others were given. A cup of soup instead of a bowl, one slice of bread instead of the two the others were handed. Alice had been right—they were trying to break her spirit through her body.

Once back in the cellar, Alice came over to Paige's mat. She wrote on the slate, repeating her offer to teach Paige how to sign and learn the language that enabled Alice to communicate easily with Mary. But the kind gesture only made Paige more depressed. By being locked up, held captive, she had lost her chance to learn lipreading at the Sinclair Institute in Scotland.

Paige turned all this over in her mind, then said to Alice, "That's very kind of you, but I won't be here very long. I'm sure my family is looking for me right now."

Alice simply gave her a doubtful look.

"How did you come to be here?" Paige asked.

Alice wrote on the slate: *My stepmother.*

Paige was taken aback. "Did she know how you would be treated here?"

Alice shook her head and wrote: *I don't think so. Other parts of this house are nice. Give a good impression. Both the Brimleys, Nettie and Horace, can put on a good show.*

"Can't you get word to them? Your stepmother? Surely your father? Tell them what is going on?"

Alice shrugged.

"Don't they ever come to see you?" Paige persisted.

*My father would if he could* was what Paige read on the slate. She was afraid to probe any further. Alice's eyes showed how deep her hurt was.

"What about the others?"

It took Alice a long time to print out the explanation. So long, in fact, that Paige began to think it might be a good idea to learn at least a few signs in order to communicate more quickly with Alice and Mary.

*Jeremy and Tom are brothers, both blind. Parents are missionaries overseas. Grandparents too old, feeble to take care of them.*

"What about Mary?"

*Mary's mother died when she was a baby. She has two older sisters. Both married, with families of their own. When they found out she was deaf, they put her in a deaf school. That's how she learned signing. She was brought here by her oldest sister.*

*The boys are better off than the rest of us. They can play music. Tom the harmonica and Jeremy the concertina. Their cups are usually full. That's about all I know. Too tired at night to talk much.*

It was a tedious task for Alice to write down all this information. As she finished each sentence, she handed it to Paige to read, then she erased it and wrote the next.

Paige was appalled at what she was learning. "It's criminal what they're doing. When my family finds out about this, they'll do something, I'm sure."

Alice sighed. Paige reached out and gave her a spontaneous hug. How thin the girl was. Paige could feel her bones through her dress, her body as tiny and fragile as a little bird.

Impulsively Paige promised, "We'll find a way to get out of here. I'll get you out, Alice. You and Mary and the boys too."

Alice didn't respond. She looked tired from her long day out on the streets. She stifled a yawn and gave a little wave, then went to her mat and was soon asleep.

But Paige lay awake, every nerve tingling, her mind seething with what Alice had told her. She was finally beginning to grasp the situation here. It was some sort of subversive operation where families, for whatever reason, placed their handicapped children. Paige wanted to give these families the benefit of the doubt; these placements may have been misrepresented to the families. No humane adult could knowingly put a child in this kind of cruel confinement.

However, that did not explain her own abduction. Unless—and this thought chilled her—was Alistair Sinclair somehow involved in this? Did he arrange for wealthy clients to pay exorbitant fees in some kind of bogus scheme? No! Not possible. Paige remembered his truthful eyes, his sincere manner. No, surely her suspicions were just a result of her terrible experience. The lack of food, water, light, and air had somehow dulled her ability to think logically. No, Dr. Sinclair could be in no way connected with this band of criminals. But maybe some sort of a mastermind had conceived this plan to exploit the helpless such as her fellow captives. Maybe the Brimleys were only collecting the money and paying off someone else.

The more Paige thought about this, the more determined she became. She had to devise a plan to escape and to lead the others out too. With God's help! Paige had been made to memorize Scriptures as a child, but unfortunately, only fragments of them came to comfort her now. One, however, seemed to reassure her, Psalm 46:1: "God is our refuge and strength, a very present help in trouble." She searched her memory for the line that followed and discovered it was harder to apply: "Therefore we will not fear. . . ." *Trust.* She must trust him to help her apply this—as she had never been so afraid in her life.

*P*aige had lost track of time. The days and nights merged into each other. Daily she went upstairs with the others and managed to swallow some of the watery mess that passed for soup. In the mornings she pretended to be asleep when Nettie roused the others for their day out begging. She refused to even open her eyes when the woman stood over her, nudging her with the toe of her shoe.

Then one night Alice crept over to Paige's mat and wrote on her slate. *They're going to make you go out. I heard them talking. Horace says if that fellow doesn't make another payment for your board and keep, you'll go out with the rest of us.*

Paige was instantly alert. She took the chalk from Alice and circled the word *fellow,* then made a question mark.

*Horace didn't say the name,* Alice wrote.

Paige's heart thundered. Who was paying the Brimleys to keep her here?

She remembered when Mr. Martengale, her grandmother's lawyer, had learned of her engagement to Charles. He had insisted on drawing up a prenuptial agreement for them to sign. When she had protested, he told her, "You have no idea of the size of your inheritance. Unless protected, it will be completely transferred to your husband. That is why your mother wanted her own American attorney to safeguard your future."

Of course, Paige trusted Charles. She had not even read the documents she had signed—all that small print. However, a few stipulations came to mind now. Something about a sum to be paid to Charles if any physical, mental, or emotional "impediment" to the marriage was apparent before the union took place. Would her deafness be considered an impediment? Did Charles want out of his commitment? Had he plotted to have her whisked away, seemingly disoriented, irrational, so that he could be released from their engagement and then benefit financially?

No! No! No! Paige refused to believe such treachery.

She didn't remember falling asleep that night. The next thing she was aware of was waking stiff and aching, headachy and hungry. Then she felt the vibration of Nettie's heavy footsteps clunking down the stairway into the cellar.

Paige shut her eyes, squeezing them tightly, not wanting to wake up to the reality of her situation. She was used to waking under a downy quilt in a warm room, bright with a newly lighted fire. Flora would appear like magic with a tray upon which a silver pot held fragrant tea and a covered dish contained freshly baked scones. Now she was being shaken by a bone-bruising grip on her shoulders.

Nettie stood over her, shouting and throwing a bundle of clothes at her, indicating she should put them on.

Paige tossed the clothes back at her. "I will not."

Nettie shouted something else, and although Paige could not hear the exact words, she guessed they contained some kind of threat, probably along the lines Alice had predicted. "If you want to eat, you'd better."

For the next two days Paige stubbornly refused to go out. Each morning the confrontation with Nettie got worse. Her face was always blotched and red, and her mouth twisted as she hurled vicious words at Paige.

Paige remained all day and night in the cellar. Alice would bring her bread from her own meager provision, and she got water from the rusty faucet outside the cellar in the small courtyard next to the privy. A grill was clamped tightly over the tiny space in case anyone thought of trying to escape that way.

Her stomach growled constantly, and she could feel herself growing hungrier and weaker with each passing day. Paige was determined to hold out and not let the Brimleys break her.

However, even as she continued to ignore Nettie's rantings and threats, Paige came to believe that her best move might be to pretend to give up. Go along. Maybe use going out with the others to good advantage. Wasn't sending her out to beg a risk? Weren't they afraid she'd run away, get help? It seemed a foolish thing for them to do. These were criminals, yet not all criminals were clever. Paige had no idea exactly where they were or where they took their victims to beg. Alice did not know either. She told Paige they were placed in different locations every day. If Paige went along, would she be able to figure it out? The more she thought about it, the more she knew she wanted to try, if for no other reason than to find out how Nettie and Horace operated.

After coming to that conclusion, Paige made a great pretense of acting shaky and subdued when Nettie came down the following morning and began her usual tirade. Then slowly, as if it were a great effort, Paige unbuttoned the jacket of her fashionable blue traveling suit with its velvet trim. It was wrinkled from sleeping in it on a moldy pallet on a filthy floor. As she took it off, Nettie stood, her fat arms folded across her chest, and watched with smug satisfaction. She pointed to Paige's ruffled petticoat.

Paige unfastened the drawstring around her waist. The tiered, lace-trimmed undergarment dropped, and she stepped out of it. She pulled the dress out of the sack thrown at her days ago and shook it out. It smelled as though it had been bunched up in some musty trunk for years. The bodice was stained and mended, the skirt full of patches.

Nettie picked up Paige's fine leather, French-heeled boots and then flung their substitutes down on the mat and pointed to them.

Paige looked at the replacement shoes. The leather was scuffed and worn, the uppers cracked. The sole on one was coming loose and was tied with an old string to keep it together. Paige knew she couldn't go far in those. Maybe that was the point. Maybe her captors anticipated she might try to make a run for it and were taking this precaution. It only stiffened her resolve to outwit them.

Anger rushed up again, and she was tempted to rebel. But to spend another day in solitary confinement in this dungeon? How long could she hold out? She looked over at Alice and scrawny little Mary. With an involuntary sting of tears, Paige realized they were all in this together. If the others were reaping any kind of retribution from her sowing, she owed them. It was up to Paige to find a way out for all of them.

While Paige got into the shabby outfit, Nettie yelled at the others and hustled them to roll up their mats and fold their blankets.

When Paige was fully dressed in her begging clothes, she looked down at herself. She bit her lip to keep from crying. Dressed in those clothes, she actually felt like a ragamuffin—inferior, humiliated, ashamed. Of course, this was exactly how these criminals wanted her and the others to feel and to look. Paige had to control her furious indignation as Nettie pushed them all into line and up the stairs, down the hall and into the kitchen.

Horace stood by the huge, black stove, drinking a mug of tea. It was the first time Paige had seen him since the day of her kidnapping. As they took their places at the table, he gave them all a sour look from under heavy-lidded eyes, then he said something to Nettie.

Nettie moved her mouth like a clapper and jerked her head toward Paige. Horace then threw Paige a mean glance, snarling something in return. Nettie slopped thin gruel into bowls and passed them down the table. Paige managed to get a little down; it was tasteless and had the consistency of glue, but she knew its sustenance had to last all day. She kept reminding herself she had to keep her wits about her, be sharp, observe, and remember everything. The route they took, so as to be able to retrace it if necessary, the location of shops or buildings around the corner where Horace Brimley left them to beg.

They were hardly given time to gulp down half a mug of weak tea before they were hustled along the hall and down the porch steps. It was still dark outside. They were quickly herded into what looked like the same wagon Horace and Nettie had thrown Paige into on her ride here from the railroad station. There were no windows and no seats, so all they could do was bounce and rattle around in the vehicle for what seemed a long distance. Finally it lurched to a stop, and a few minutes later the back doors opened.

Horace lifted the two boys out of the wagon, then put a wooden crate down for them to sit on and handed them their musical instruments. He slung their placards over their heads. Blind Boys, No Home, No Food, Will Play For Pennies.

Paige seethed. This was truly a crime. Didn't anyone see that? Where were the much-praised "bobbies"—the policemen of whom London was so proud? These child abusers were operating right under their noses and should be arrested. How could such evil exist in plain sight?

Of course, Paige knew she was hopelessly naive. In a city like London there were warrens of slums, a complete underworld thriving beneath the surface. She had simply never been exposed to it before.

The sections of London that housed the class of society to which Paige belonged, where the wealthy shopped and dined and attended theater, were swept clean of the sight of ragged children and poverty. She was learning fast that not everyone was as well fed, well housed, and well cared for as she had always been.

After settling the boys, Horace banged the doors shut and took off again. It was another long, jolting ride until the wagon stopped. The doors were thrown open once again, and Horace jerked his thumb for Alice, Mary, and Paige to get out. As they stepped down from the wagon, Paige could see that they were at a fairly busy intersection. Horace took another wooden crate and a few stools and set them up on the corner a few feet away. He pointed to the girls and gave them an order. Paige didn't need to know lipreading to understand, "Sit!" They might as well have been dogs. Alice and Mary sat, but Paige remained standing. He looked at her, then reached into the wagon and grabbed a placard strung on yarn. He tossed it over her head. She turned it up to read the crudely printed sign. Deaf and Dumb.

He put his face close to hers and waggled his finger with its dirty nail under her nose. Then he quickly took a piece of coal out of his pocket, rubbed his hands on it, and smeared her cheeks. He did the same to Alice and Mary.

Paige patted her skirt for a pocket, hoping to find a handkerchief, but her skirt had no pockets. The oft-repeated admonition of her governess flashed into her mind: "A lady *always* carries a dainty lace-trimmed handkerchief with her." She almost laughed. Poor Miss Boles would need smelling salts if she could see her former student now.

Horace gave Paige another dark look and snarled something, not seeming to care that she could not hear his threat, then turned on his heel and got back in the wagon. Paige watched it rattle down the street until it rounded the corner.

Paige immediately looked around the intersection for any possibility of escape. It was a rather downtrodden neighborhood—several pubs, a pawnshop, a shabby storefront or two. Mostly it looked like a row of warehouses. Maybe this was a testing place for her first day out. Paige didn't think the three of them would receive many contributions hereabouts unless some of the tavern patrons, their brains addled with too much drink, emptied their pockets as they wobbled out.

Resigned to the fact that she couldn't do anything at the moment, Paige sat huddled closely for warmth between little Mary and Alice. She had no idea where they were. Nothing seemed familiar. Tall, ugly, smoke-stained brick buildings towered all around them. She saw no sign of a policeman or anyone from whom they might seek help.

This first day on the streets as a beggar was unbelievably long for Paige. The sky was overcast and threatened rain, and as the day wore on, it got colder and darker. Hunched people hurried by them, surely eager to get home to a cozy fire and a hot cup of tea. Not many stopped long enough to throw a few coins at the two younger girls holding up their cups. Paige absolutely refused to beg, even though she suspected that the punishment for not having anything to show for her day would be swift and harsh.

She was right. When Horace Brimley returned to pick them up at the end of the day, he examined each of their cups. When he saw that Paige's was empty, he jerked her roughly to her feet, his mouth twisted and snarling something. It was not hard to tell where he had spent the day; his breath was hot and smelled heavily of ale.

Back at the house, Nettie dealt out her own particular brand of vengeance. Paige received only one small potato and no bread with the watery stew that was called supper that evening.

*T*he next day the same dreary routine took place. They were routed out of bed at daybreak and given a poor excuse for a breakfast, then trundled into the wagon. Alice, Mary, and Paige were let out first that day. Before handing her the battered tin begging cup, Horace had parting words for her. Without hearing them, Paige knew once again that they were some kind of threat.

After the wagon drove away, Paige settled in beside the other two girls but refused to hold out her cup. She had already made up her mind that this would be the day she would find a way to get help. Again they had been placed at a thoroughfare that was in a run-down section. No one of her own social standing was likely to be familiar with such a neighborhood. However, she still tried to stop passersby with her story. She would grab a coat sleeve or a skirt, desperately trying to get someone to listen.

"Please, get in touch with my grandmother. I'll give you her address. Tell her I've been kidnapped, that I'm being held against my will—"

Paige soon gave up; it was no use. The women would simply look at her with frightened eyes, pull away, and hurry off down the street without looking back. Men would shake off her clinging hands, frowning and increasing their pace. They may have thought she was an escapee from the insane asylum. And who could blame them? A few weeks ago she might have thought the same thing if someone who looked like she did now—hair uncombed, face blackened, wild-eyed—had attempted to stop them with some crazy tale about being kidnapped. Paige decided to abandon that plan. Someone could too easily notify the authorities, and then maybe she would end up in an asylum.

Worse still, everyone was in such a hurry to get away from her that they would not even stop long enough to drop a coin into the other two girls' cups.

As the day wore on, it got colder. Gusts of chill wind blew loose pages of newspapers and assorted trash down through the alleyway and into the street. People clutched their hat brims or drew their thin shawls tighter and passed the girls without a glance. The girls huddled together while it grew darker still. By the time Brimley showed up, Paige was freezing and furious. When he picked up their cups, Paige realized Alice had slipped a few of her own coins into her cup, surely trying to save Paige from more punishment. However, the day's take was lean, and Horace was in a foul mood. He pushed them all roughly into the wagon. Paige's anger kept brewing, fueling itself into fury. When the wagon finally stopped and they got out, Horace shoved the two boys up the porch steps and into the house. Paige had had enough. She whirled around and confronted him. "Don't think you can get away with doing this to me and these poor, helpless children. Wait until my relatives hear about this! They'll call the police."

Horace's lips curled, and he sneered something that of course she couldn't hear. It must have been serious, though, for at that point Alice quickly tugged at her arm, warning her.

Paige gave Horace what she hoped was a scathing look. But then she realized he might take his anger out on the others, and so she said no more. She simply lifted her chin defiantly and started walking away.

Just then Nettie appeared at the kitchen door. She spoke to Horace, and he answered, motioning to Paige as he did so.

Nettie shook her wooden spoon and made a swatting gesture toward Paige as if she were going to hit her. Paige ducked and stepped back.

Later, back in the cellar, she asked Alice, "What did Horace say when I told him my relatives would have the police after him?"

Alice looked worried, then wrote on the slate: *He said it was your relatives who put you here.*

Stunned, Paige stared at Alice. "You mean like your stepmother brought you?"

Alice nodded and wrote: *I guess. I don't know.*

"But I was kidnapped, Alice! They grabbed me on the street. I was at the railroad station with my cousin. Are you *sure* that's what he said?"

Alice nodded again, and her eyes clouded with tears. She wrote: *I'm sorry, if it is true.*

"I don't believe him," Paige said.

Was he lying or just being cruel? Was it possible? Alice had written on the slate once that she thought Mary's family couldn't accept her deafness and so had sent her here. Paige felt sick. Could someone have arranged this?

Or was it just another sadistic way Horace used to torture his victims? Her case *was* different from either Mary's, Alice's, or the boys' . . . wasn't it? Surely by now someone would have declared her missing, started a search . . .

That night, as she lay sleepless and churning with anger, Paige came to a decision. She *must* figure out some way to escape. She had read how prisoners in the Bastille during the French Revolution kept themselves sane by plotting elaborate escape schemes. She had to stay strong and not buckle under the pressure of these terrible people. . . . She had to think carefully, plan carefully.

She could start by saving some money out of her cup, just a few pennies at a time, just enough to hail a passing hansom cab or get to a police station or maybe an omnibus stop. Was Horace telling the truth when he claimed to have spies watching them while they were left to beg on the streets? Probably for a few shillings he could get some down-on-his-luck derelict to be a lookout. Her escape would have to be swift and unexpected.

Paige tried to settle down and get some rest, knowing the next day would be as awful and as grueling as this one, but her mind was too restless, too crowded with memories. The memories were the most painful—those of Thatcher, all they had shared, carefree times of happiness and laughter. Charles came to mind next, and their future hopes and dreams. A wave of melancholy swept over her. She had never appreciated her life, had taken everything for granted, had been so sheltered, used to abundance and luxury. Paige had given little thought to the street people, the homeless, the help-less, the neglected, rejected, or exploited. Nor had she thought about the cruelty of poverty. Until she lost her hearing, she had never come face-to-face with anything that threatened her comfortable, pampered way of life.

Paige had never even prayed very much. She had had everything she needed and had never known what it was like to be helpless. A desperate kind of prayer rose from the depth of her despairing heart now. "If I ever get out of here, I *will* be different. I *will* do something to change things. Forgive me for all I neglected in the past, Lord. Please, help me, give me a sign, some direction of what I should do."

Just then Alice crept over to her side. She held up her slate so that by the light of the sputtering candle Paige could read what she had written: *Are you ready to learn signing?*

Paige almost laughed. The Lord was certainly answering quickly. She hugged Alice and whispered, "Yes, Alice, yes, I think that's a splendid idea."

*I*ncredibly, the seeming hopelessness of her situation began to give Paige a stubborn strength. For all their cruelty, the Brimleys were stupid to think they could get away with something like this. She still had no idea how long she had been held captive, no way of telling time—one dreary day followed another. But along with her new resolve, she had a growing faith that God would answer her prayer and give her a plan, a way to escape. And a way to get the others out of here too. Now that Paige knew this kind of horror existed, she would never forget it. There must be dozens of such victims hidden all over the city of London in dank cellars and dusty attics, exploited and shamefully neglected.

The days of begging in the cold, wind, and rain were miserable. Left in a strange part of town, a different place every day, Paige could not tell how far they were from the city of London itself, nor did she know the location of the Brimleys' prison house. To pass the time, they practiced signing, and she was learning fast. She tried to forget her missed opportunity at the Sinclair Institute. Right now signing was all she had, and it might enable her escape.

She began to hold some money back from the little she received each day. Alice and Mary, appealing little girls, garnered more attention and so collected more coins in their cups. Paige figured all they needed was the price of three tickets to catch an omnibus or even to persuade a hansom cabbie to take them all to Mallory Hall.

One day it began to pour, and they had nothing with which to shelter themselves. The jutting overhang of the building where they were stationed was not wide enough to shield them from the downpour, and the building's rotted drainpipe leaked like a sieve, dripping water continually. By the time Horace finally returned, the girls were soaked to the skin, their threadbare clothes sodden. Paige was so furious she didn't care what the repercussions would be. Hugging the frail little Mary, whose teeth were chattering, she railed at Horace. "What kind of man are you, leaving us out here in all this rain for hours? Can't you see this child is drenched? Where have you been? Holed up in a nice, warm pub drinking a couple of pints, I suspect. You should be horsewhipped."

Paige saw she had hit the mark. His face turned red, almost purple, with fury.

Her arms still around Mary, she wasted no more time berating Horace. The sooner this child got out of her wet clothes, got wrapped in a blanket, and was given something hot to drink, the better. The three of them scrambled into the back of the wagon, where Jeremy and Tom were already huddled together. Horace slammed the doors shut.

When they got back to the house, Paige hurried into the kitchen. Nettie stood at the stove.

"Put some water on to boil immediately," she ordered. "And get some warm clothes for Mary to change into." Astonished at Paige's assertiveness, Nettie stood like a statue. *"Now,"* Paige said, "unless you want to have a child dying of pneumonia on your hands. That would be pretty hard to explain to her family, to say nothing of the police."

Paige sensed movement behind her and turned to see Horace coming unsteadily toward her. She ignored him and turned back to Nettie. "*Do* it."

Some kind of verbal exchange took place between him and Nettie. Nettie's mouth moved angrily, and Horace stumbled over to a chair and dropped onto it, head lolling drunkenly. He took out a red handkerchief and wiped his sweating face.

Paige helped Mary out of her soaked dress. Then she grabbed Nettie's shawl, which was hanging over a chair, and draped it tightly around the shivering little girl.

For some reason, Nettie followed Paige's directions. Then, while Paige held a cup, Nettie filled it with hot tea for Mary to sip. "Alice needs dry things too," she told Nettie.

At this Nettie regained a little of her usual belligerent manner and sneered something back at Paige.

Paige answered coldly, "You would do well to do what I'm telling you. You and he," she pointed to Horace, "are going to be in enough trouble when I expose you to the authorities."

At this statement, Horace rose with such violence that his chair fell over backwards. Infuriated as well as drunk, Horace took a few steps toward Paige with doubled fists. But he was so unsteady on his feet that he stumbled against the table.

Nettie gave him a disgusted look, then went to the closet. She pulled out a blanket and an assortment of clothes and thrust them at Paige.

Paige felt Mary's forehead and cheeks; they were hot to the touch. Even the sullen Nettie looked a little worried.

"Mary is very sick," Paige told her. "She has a fever. Unless you want to explain a child dead of pneumonia, put her in a decent bed and take care of her."

Nettie's mouth opened as if she were about to make some angry rebuttal, but after only a second's hesitation, she nodded.

Mary weighed next to nothing when Alice and Paige picked her up and followed Nettie through another doorway into a part of the house Paige had never seen. Alice and Paige exchanged a look. It was, as Alice had told her, a nicely furnished house that one might find in any middle-class neighborhood. So this was the "front" shown to relatives who came here to place their crippled, blind, or otherwise handicapped relative. Anyone could easily assume it would be a comfortable, pleasant home in which to put the unwanted one. This particular room was high ceilinged, with a shiny, brass bed in the center piled with pillows and a quilt. There was a fireplace in the corner. They lay Mary on the bed and covered her. Paige gave Nettie a contemptuous look. It enraged Paige even more to see this part of the house and then consider the conditions in which Mary and the others were confined.

Nettie avoided eye contact and motioned for the two girls to leave. Paige refused. "I'll stay with her through the night. She'll need to be watched carefully, or you may have to call a doctor. Then I believe you'll have some explaining to do."

Nettie looked scared. Even if Mary wasn't gravely ill, Paige had frightened Nettie over what the dire consequences might be if Mary were neglected.

Alice looked at Paige with admiration before Nettie ushered her out of the bedroom. Left alone with Mary, Paige took off her own wet dress and hung it to dry near the fire that Nettie had lit before she left the room. During that long night, Paige checked on Mary frequently, wondering how the rest of them could use her illness to their benefit. Would the Brimleys call in a doctor if she got worse?

Perhaps. By morning Mary's breathing was more even, but she had developed a hoarse cough. When Nettie appeared, Paige simply told her Mary was too sick to go out, and she better take good care of her.

Alice and Paige followed Horace out to the wagon as usual. He seemed to have a bad hangover from the previous day's

Indulgence. He was puffy eyed, splotchy faced, and meaner than ever. After dropping them off, he got back in the wagon and, instead of disappearing around his usual corner, he pulled to a stop in front of a pub down the street. A minute later he disappeared inside.

"This may be our chance," Paige told Alice. "He's gone to drink some more, and he'll be fuzzy headed and slow when he comes out. Maybe we can get away."

*But how?* Alice signed. Paige was now grateful Alice had taught her some signs; it made communication so much easier and faster.

"All we need is the price of an omnibus ticket. It will get us somewhere, and maybe we can find someone who will believe us and get word to my grandmother."

*Do you really think we can?* Alice signed.

"We have to try. You were right. The rest of the house would mislead anyone. You saw the nice room Nettie put Mary in. It's a sin how they keep us down in the cellar! It's criminal."

The weather that day was miserable, with fog and drizzle. This was not a busy day; hardly anybody ventured out on foot. There were no signs of an omnibus on a regular route. Only a few carriages and an occasional hansom cab went by. Paige counted only a few coppers in the cup Alice held in her hands.

Paige kept her eyes glued on the pub, watching for Horace to come out. As the morning wore on, he still had not appeared. Her spirits lifted. The longer he stayed, the more he drank, and the better their chances of getting away.

Realistically, without transportation and considering the shoddy shoes they'd been given to wear, Paige knew they couldn't get very far very fast.

Toward midday it began to rain. Not hard, just steadily enough to chill the bones. This time a building nearby happened to have overhanging eaves, so they moved their stools and box underneath for shelter. The rain continued. The pavement became riddled with puddles, and they pushed their box and stools farther back, closer to the building. A newspaper that had dropped from a passing vehicle blew across the street and plastered itself against the lamppost. Paige dashed to retrieve it, thinking it might provide some cover from the wind-driven rain needling them. However, it was too tattered and sodden to provide any shelter. The ink was blurred, but she could just make out today's date. Three weeks had passed since her kidnapping! How had she lost track of so much time? She'd read how prisoners marked the days off on the walls of their cells. She groaned.

Alice looked at her with worried eyes. *What is it?* she signed.

"I just realized how long I've been here. My grandmother must be sick with worry. I *must* get home or get word to her somehow . . . and Charles, my fiancé, has no idea where I am. Neither does Thatcher, my dearest friend . . ." Paige clutched Alice's arm. "We must get away from the Brimleys, Alice! Report them to the police. We *have* to—"

She looked once more in the direction of the pub, and this time she saw Horace come out, weaving back and forth as he made his way to the wagon.

A fierce anger at the dreadful man rushed up inside of her. Whatever it took, she would escape. What could he do? Kill her?

She grabbed Alice's arms. "Come on, Alice. We won't let him stuff us in that thing one more time. We'll run. Go to the nearest police station . . ."

She jumped up, pulling Alice with her, overturning the stools and the wooden crate. One of the stools clattered into the street, alerting Horace. When he saw them start to run, he stumbled across the intersection in pursuit. He had his driving whip in one hand and started waving it at them. With the amount of drink he had probably consumed, certainly he would not hesitate to use it.

Paige glanced at Alice lagging behind as they hurried down the street. She was quivering, her shoulders hunched as if already warding off the cutting lashes. In a flash Paige knew they would not make it. They were both too handicapped. With her withered leg, Alice could not run.

Alice halted, panting. "*You* go on, Paige," she signed frantically.

Under no circumstances would Paige leave Alice to that brute. She halted, put her arm protectively around Alice, and then turned to face Horace. As he approached them, she could see that he'd wrapped the length of the whip around one hand but still had a firm grip on the handle. He looked nervously around him, then snarled something and jerked his head in the direction of the wagon. Alice clung to Paige. They had no alternative but to obey. With a defiant glare, Paige followed Alice to the wagon where they scrambled inside, knowing Horace would shove them in if they didn't hurry. He was still ranting things Paige was glad she couldn't hear when he slammed and locked the wagon doors.

Inside Alice hugged her then signed, *I'm scared. He said he was going to teach you a lesson you wouldn't forget.*

They stopped to pick up the boys, then rattled on their way. *Faster than usual,* Paige thought. She dreaded what lay ahead. Her one attempt to save them had failed. She had failed. In that lost opportunity everything else, even Horace's present threats, seemed unimportant.

Once he had hustled them into the house, Horace wasted no time carrying out his threat. He pulled Paige away from Alice and flung her against the wall. His small, pig eyes squinted, and his face twisted into a hideous mask of fury as he moved toward her menacingly. He continued to draw closer while Tom, Jeremy, and Alice shrank back.

A streak of fear shot up and raced through Paige's body. She knew he wanted her to cringe and cower, but she was determined not to. She thrust out her chin.

"You despicable man," she said. "Don't you dare strike me! You'll be sorry if you lay a finger on me. My grandmother will have you punished as you deserve to be when she finds out how you've treated me and the others."

She started to turn away, but then she felt herself being spun around. With his hamlike hands Horace cuffed her hard on both sides of her head. Dizzily Paige tried to get away from him, but he took hold of her hair and yanked her around. He raised his hand to hit her again, and she ducked so that the blow landed on her ear. Paige felt a ringing pain and saw an explosion of stars. Her knees sagged, and she staggered. She would have sunk to the floor if he had not jerked her to her feet right then. Holding her by her arm, he dragged her, stumbling, along the hallway to the cellar door. He yanked it open and threw her down the stairs.

Paige bounced, her shoulders, spine, and the back of her head hitting the hard wooden steps. She rolled helplessly into the yawning darkness.

*13*

aige slowly opened her eyes as the flame of a flickering candle was passed back and forth over her. She tried to see who was holding it, but her vision was blurred. She tried to lift her head, but the pain was too sharp—so intense that her whole skull throbbed. She closed her eyes again; even her eyelids hurt. How long had she been unconscious?

Paige became dimly aware of a soft sobbing. Was she dreaming, or did she actually *hear* it? She attempted to move but winced. Every bone and joint felt bruised and sore. Paige made the effort to raise herself but it was too much. She fell back with a moan, closing her eyes again.

She felt a small, warm hand smoothing back her hair from her forehead and heard little mewing sounds. Someone was leaning over her.

"Poor, poor Paige."

Her eyes flew open. She knew it was Alice even though she'd never heard her voice before.

"I'm so sorry, Paige," Alice said in a tearful voice, "Horace is such a beast . . ."

In spite of aching all over, Paige reached up and took Alice's gentle hand. She didn't trust herself to tell her friend of her discovery. It was too overwhelming. She drew a painful breath. Were her ribs broken? Then she heard Alice sniffle and say her name again. She *heard* it, softly, as Alice said it. She *did* hear it. It was true. Somehow, miraculously, the blows had restored her hearing. Paige ran her tongue across her dry lips and swallowed hard as she tried to speak. Finally she was able to manage a hoarse whisper.

"Alice, listen, something wonderful has happened. I can hear you. Imagine! Horace's hitting me and pushing me down the steps has somehow—I don't know how, but—all I know is that I can *hear* you. Hear as well as I ever did!"

It took some convincing to assure Alice that a miracle had happened. Then they began talking in excited whispers, marveling at the fact that Horace's vicious blows had brought this about.

"As soon as I can move we must get out of here, Alice," Paige told her urgently. "You and I are best able to do it and that way help the others. First of all, let's keep the fact that I can hear a secret. Only you and I will know. That way I can gather information and evidence about who is behind all of this. The Brimleys aren't smart enough to have thought up this whole scheme by themselves. There's some mastermind behind this. Here's what we'll do: We'll go on as before. Horace will think he has intimidated me, and I'll let him think so. But we'll wait for our chance. We'll check out the streets every time he leaves us and remember the one closest to an omnibus stop. We'll keep back some of the money each day, and the right time will come. We'll know when it's right." *With God's help,* Paige added to herself. She wasn't sure, after all of her months here in this prison, if Alice still trusted God.

Alice looked scared. "I don't know . . . I never thought there'd be a way out—"

Paige grabbed Alice's hands and squeezed them. "You have to believe there is. You aren't doomed to spend your life like this, Alice. None of the others are, either. We've just got to be brave and believe it. I promise I won't go without you."

They hugged then, and Alice finally went back to her own mat and slept.

But Paige could not sleep. The marvel of her restored hearing was still taking hold. She knew she had a difficult task ahead. Much would be demanded of her. She would be tested as she had never been tested before. She must be physically strong and morally brave.

As she lay there in the darkness, she renewed her prayer and her promise. "Lord, if you help me escape, I *will* change. I *will* be different. You have let me see myself as I never have before. And I will help not only these four, but I'll do something beyond that, something positive with my life. Just give me a chance to prove it."

The next morning when Nettie came into the cellar, stood next to her mat, and looked down at her, Paige pretended to be asleep.

Nettie nudged Paige with the toe of her house-slippered foot, probably just to assure herself that Paige wasn't dead. Paige was tempted to hold her breath and try to give the wretched woman a good scare.

Nettie went back to the foot of the steps. "She ain't awake," she hollered up to the open door where Horace stood, "but her face is swollen and bruised. Jest yer dumb luck ya didn't kill her, 'Orace. Ya best keep off the juice or things could get a lot worse. Don't forget them people are comin' in a few days. Ya better be in shape and be sharp. He's a sly one iffen you arsk me. Could put one over on ya if ya don't keep your wits about ya."

Horace gave a grunt and turned back, letting the door bang behind him.

Paige wasn't used to hearing again. But eavesdropping on these two would certainly prove useful. Who was it they were expecting? And did this person have something to do with this terrible scheme the Brimleys were working? She promised herself she would find out. Paige remained motionless on her mat and did not stir while Nettie rousted the others out to get them off to their day of begging.

Before Alice left, she slipped over to Paige and whispered that she would check on Mary and bring back any news of what was happening upstairs.

After hearing that snatch of conversation between the Brimleys, Paige wondered what had taken place after Horace's attack on her. Had they quarreled?

When the wagon was gone, the house settled into silence. Paige heard it roll away and knew Horace had taken her fellow captives off to another miserable day on the streets. But not for too many more days, God willing.

After a while she heard the floorboards creaking under Nettie's considerable weight as she went about her daily chores. Paige pondered how she might catch the two criminals red-handed and expose their fraud. How had they managed to mislead people into believing that this was a respectable and compassionate home for the disabled? Paige just could not believe that everyone who brought a handicapped relative here did it with evil intent. Some must have thought this was at least a safe haven from a world that might not accept them. Tom and Jeremy's parents, for example, were self-sacrificing missionaries who must have felt they were putting their boys in a safe, secure place while they were away. The Brimleys must have been better actors than Paige had given them credit for to have convinced the God-fearing couple that they would take good care of their blind sons.

Two days passed before Paige could move without involuntarily moaning with pain. She practiced walking across the cellar until some flexibility returned. She needed her mobility at its best for that moment when she would be back at the begging post and the opportunity arose to escape.

On the third day Paige was exercising her muscles—stretching her arms and swinging her legs—when she heard the peal of the doorbell. Someone was coming to the house!

She crept to the top of the stairs and crouched there, her ear pressed against the door, listening.

Paige heard the murmur of voices—Nettie's and another man's and woman's—speaking in casual tones. Nettie's voice seemed false, affected somehow. Evidently Nettie was entertaining this couple in the parlor. Later she heard footsteps and assumed Nettie was showing them the rest of the house—at least the part she wanted them to see.

New clients? Distraught parents desperately seeking a place to board some child or relative they could not cope with or care for themselves?

A wild impulse struck her. Should she burst on the scene and tell them the truth? Nettie was alone. Would they believe her? All Nettie could do was deny Paige's accusation and perhaps tell the prospective clients that this poor, disheveled young woman was mad. Tentatively, she turned the door handle quietly, but of course it was locked. Even so, her idea was risky. She could not count on anyone but herself. She had to get completely away, had to get Alice out of harm's way, before exposing the Brimleys.

Paige heard the sound of a carriage and horses' hooves outside. She limped down the steps and over to one of the high windows, where she stood on tiptoe, her eyes barely topping the windowsill. A man in a cape and top hat, his back to her, helped a woman into a hansom cab. Nettie's bulk blocked her view of the woman. Paige longed to bang on the window to attract their attention, but she knew it was futile. She watched the vehicle disappear down the road.

That evening Alice brought Paige some bread and a cup of watery broth. "They were talking about you. Horace said it was time you were out and working again."

"He's right," Paige agreed grimly. "The sooner the better. We can't wait much longer, Alice."

"He said something else."

"What?"

Alice looked embarrassed. "Well, Nettie said something about you being a different case. And he got real mad. He said, 'As fer as I can see she ain't no differ'nt than the rest of them freaks . . . can't hear, can't talk, can't walk, all crips and dummies. Don't nobody want 'em around, most of all folks like her high-and-mighty family. Why else would they pay good money to put her away?'"

Paige drew in her breath sharply. "And what did Nettie say to that?"

"She said, 'Don't forget there's more in it for us with her, 'Orace. That's what he told us. He just wants a little more time. Yer lucky it ain't any sooner. Them bruises ya give her aren't pretty. We don't want no questions. Whatever the game is, the less we know, the better off we be. Best to go along till we got the cash in hand.'"

Alice was a superb mimic. Paige smiled at her accurate imitation of Nettie. She reached over and patted Alice's hand.

"Don't worry, Alice. I'm planning something, and we'll get out of here soon." Paige tried to sound more convincing than she actually felt. The Brimleys were awful people, but Paige didn't think either of them wanted to go to jail. Someone was paying them off. Who and why? She had to find out.

That night as Paige lay awake working out various escape plans, she became aware of loud voices overhead.

She got up as fast as she could, moved quickly over to the steps, and mounted them quietly. She pressed her ear to the door and listened.

"We 'aven't got another payment for *that 'un* since the first time. You said the next one'd come in a week." It was Horace's voice sounding belligerent.

Paige held her breath.

"You've got to give them time to be really upset," came another voice.

"How long will that take?"

"Be patient, Horace, these things take finesse." It was a man's voice, that of an upper-class Englishman.

Why was he doing business with the likes of the Brimleys?

"The money will come, I assure you, when they're convinced her disappearance wasn't voluntary."

"That better be soon. That 'un's more trouble than she's worth fer shure."

More was said, but the words were muffled, and Paige couldn't make any more sense out of the conversation. Some time later, she heard carriage wheels outside and the whinny of a horse. She couldn't try to look out because Jeremy's and Tom's pallets were right under the windows. She crept back up to the top of the steps and tried to listen again. Maybe now that their visitor had departed, the Brimleys might say something that would help her piece the puzzle together.

She waited, and sure enough they did. She heard Horace mumble something. Nettie replied, "Well, it's a good thing her family hasn't paid up to get her back yet. I wouldn't want nobody to see her like she's looking now. No thanks to ya, 'Orace. She's got a black-and-blue mark down one side of her face."

"And she deserved it, if yer arskin' me! Got a smart mouth, she 'as, and if I'd let her get away with it, she'd 'ave worked the others up too."

"Oh, shut up, 'Orace. It were a stupid thing to do, hittin' her like that."

Horace's reply was unintelligible. Silence followed. Then all Paige heard was the creak of the stairway as the Brimleys went to bed. She went back to her mat and mulled over everything she had overheard.

She must get back to Mallory Hall. But even if she did, would they believe her story? What had Demetra told the police or her grandmother? Surely someone was searching for her. Her mind whirled.

The next night Alice brought Paige some astonishing news. The Brimleys had had a heated argument.

"They heard from the Missionary Society that Tom and Jeremy's parents are coming back to England on furlough," Alice told her.

Was this the break Paige was hoping for? What would happen if the boys told their mother and father how they had been treated, what life at the Brimleys' had been like for them during their parents' absence? And the parents? As dedicated Christians would they turn the other cheek? Forgive this despicable couple? But what about justice? Didn't justice have to be served?

"Did you find out when they'll arrive?" Paige asked Alice.

"No, but soon, I think, by the nervous way Nettie was acting."

After Alice had gone to her mat, Paige lay wide awake thinking over this new information. Was now the time to act? Or should they wait until the boys' parents came?

Alice and Paige decided the Crosbys' arrival must be imminent because of what happened right after supper the next night. Nettie seated the boys one at a time on kitchen stools, placed a bowl over each head, then proceeded to cut their hair. Never having seen anything but the opposite kind of attention paid to their appearance, Paige realized this must be in preparation for the boys' parents' arrival. The Brimleys might be so preoccupied the next day with the boys that an opportunity to escape might be possible.

While they all remained sitting at their places, watching the haircutting, Paige's gaze happened to wander to the folded newspaper at the end of the table. As she casually glanced at the top of the page, one word stood out in bold type: MISSING.

Her heart started to bang. She slid her hand along the edge of the table and with careful fingers turned the paper a little so that she could read the entire boxed article.

MISSING, Young woman, deaf, may be disoriented. £500 reward for any information concerning her whereabouts. Contact the office of Fred Newsome, Private Investigator. Post Box Number 89, London. All communications strictly confidential.

The ad was about her! She was sure of it. Who was this Fred Newsome? Who had hired him to investigate her disappearance? Whatever the source, Paige felt tremendous relief. They were looking for her!

Hope surged within her, but she realized she had no time to lose. If the Brimleys saw this ad, they would surely go after the reward. She must escape soon and get home to Mallory Hall before they could play their last card.

Later that night Alice's eyes widened as Paige told her what she'd seen in the paper.

"We must get to this Newsome's office before the Brimleys collect any money. I think maybe my grandmother and her lawyer may have been behind that ad. People use private investigators when they don't want any public attention. The last thing my grandmother would want is publicity."

Alice looked doubtful. "But," she sounded hesitant, "remember what Horace said? That your relatives had arranged for your being here? What if your grandmother doesn't want you found?"

That possibility momentarily stopped Paige. Then she quickly replied, "Oh, no, Alice, not my grandmother. She would never—" Paige halted. For some reason an odd picture invaded her mind: the monthly ritual she and her grandmother went through with Mr. Martengale, the family lawyer. She knew her grandmother deeply resented it each time. Paige's signature was required on all the cheques used to pay the bills and had to be witnessed by him. She remembered his coming into her bedroom after her illness and advising her that it might be a good idea to give someone her power of attorney until she was fully recovered. Paige had mentioned Thatcher, but he had reminded her that Thatcher was leaving the country and would be unavailable for the next few months. He then suggested Demetra.

"I understand Miss Colfax has resigned her governess position and elected to stay to support Lady Ursula during this crisis."

Paige had made the countersuggestion of Charles since they would soon be married. At that time she didn't know they would be postponing the wedding until his return from duty in Ireland.

As it turned out, neither was necessary. Paige decided she was quite capable of writing her name, even if she couldn't hear.

She remembered Mr. Martengale as being a cold, legalistic person with a thin smile and distant manner. But why had he come to mind? She quickly dismissed the idea that her grandmother had anything at all to do with her kidnapping. What would she have to gain by Paige's disappearance? Perhaps temporary control of her estate since Paige was still under the legal age of twenty-one?

"No, Alice, that's impossible," Paige said firmly. "Just be prepared when the time comes not to hesitate for a moment but to do what I tell you, all right?"

"When?" was Alice's next question.

"As soon as possible. Tomorrow, even! We'll watch and wait for our chance."

Paige was so excited she could hardly sleep that night. The next morning Nettie seemed distracted as she gave her usual raucous wake-up calls. Were the Crosbys coming today? Was the Brimleys' whole flimsy house of cards about to collapse?

Paige could hardly resist taunting Nettie with her own plan to expose them. But she knew she had to be careful. No telling what they might do if they suspected her plan to escape. Since Horace's brutal attack, Paige had acted subdued and fearful, keeping her real feelings under tight control.

Mary's cough was still alarming enough for Nettie to keep her out of the wretched weather a few more days. So that morning, with his usual scowl and growled warnings, Horace deposited Alice and Paige alone at a corner.

It was a new corner. Nothing looked familiar, and thankfully, no pub stood across the street to tempt Horace to down a couple of pints and be near enough to keep an eye on them.

At first Paige and Alice kept up a running conversation about various plans of escape. But as the afternoon wore on, they talked less, and their hope for a chance to escape slowly evaporated. They nibbled on the dry bread Horace had given them for lunch and waited—for what, they weren't sure. Paige's mind supplied an old Scripture from memory: *Lord, show me Thy way.* She repeated it over and over.

"I don't know why Horace put us at an intersection like this one," Paige complained. "Hardly any traffic."

Not many pedestrians passed who might drop a spare penny in their cup. It was Mary's sweet, waiflike appearance that always garnered the fullest cup at the end of the day.

It was growing late and getting colder when an elegant carriage pulled to a stop in front of them. A man in a top hat stuck his head out the window and held out something in his gloved hand.

"Here, child," he called.

Paige nudged Alice, knowing her limp would elicit more sympathy and a larger donation than if she herself went.

Alice got up and went over to him, holding her cup. "God bless you, sir," she said in her sweet voice.

"And you, too, child," the man replied, then motioned his driver to move on.

Alice hobbled back to Paige, then held out the battered tin mug and gasped, "Look, Paige, look!"

Paige looked and drew a long breath. A gold coin glistened in the bottom of the cup.

"Alice, this is it, our chance," she exclaimed breathlessly. "Come on!" She grabbed Alice by the wrist.

"You mean *now?*"

"Yes, of course now. We must."

Alice looked back at the wooden carton and the two spindly stools. Paige had heard that sometimes a longtime prisoner is afraid to leave his or her cell, and she was afraid something like that was happening to Alice. But Paige couldn't let her falter. She started pulling her across the street. She had no real idea where they were, but they didn't have a minute to lose. Sometimes Horace showed up unexpectedly to check on them. They couldn't take a chance that he might do so today.

They walked faster, staying close to the buildings, always ready to duck into one of the alleyways should it become necessary, if Horace suddenly appeared. Paige knew she was moving quickly and that Alice was having a hard time keeping up. But they could rest later, when they were safe. For now they must keep going.

The string holding one of her shoes together snapped, and as the loose sole began flapping, Paige had to fight to keep from tripping. She thought she heard the sounds of traffic ahead. Maybe they were nearing a more traveled thoroughfare. The sound of her hard breathing rasped in her ears, and her heart thundered. She was sure she could hear city traffic noise. They might be near an omnibus stop or a hansom cab post.

Panic took over, and Paige began to run. Alice stumbled behind her, panting. Paige felt a stabbing pain in her side, and gasping for each breath, she finally halted for a minute. She leaned against a lamppost and tried to draw enough breath to go on.

"Alice, I'm sorry," she said with a sympathetic glance at her friend. "I know this is hard, but we've got to keep going."

Alice, flushed and breathless, just nodded. Paige tightened her hold on Alice's hand, and they continued on. In the distance Paige spotted a hansom cab.

"Come on, Alice." She quickened her steps. She could feel Alice dragging behind her, so she gripped Alice's wrist. They had to get there before he took off again.

"Hurry, Alice." Paige waved her arm wildly, signaling the cabbie to wait.

They had to cross a wide intersection. On one corner was a pub, and she felt a shiver of fear. *Don't let Horace be in it or come out as we cross the street!* she prayed.

Alice was limping badly, but they couldn't slow down now. They started across the street.

"Wait!" Paige shouted to the cabbie. "Hold on, we're coming!" As shabby as they looked, he might be tempted to ignore them. "We've got the fare!" she called out.

Almost completely out of breath, they made it to the hansom cab. The cabbie looked down at them, his expression skeptical.

"Do you know where Ashleigh is?" Paige asked breathlessly.

He nearly dropped the short pipe in his clenched mouth. "Ashleigh? That's clear out of the city, a good eighteen miles or more."

"Perhaps, but this is a matter of life or death," she told him. "We must get to my grandmother at Mallory Hall. We have the money. See!" She opened her clutched fist so he could see the gold coin.

"I dunno." The cabbie shook his head doubtfully. "How do I know you didn't snitch it? I don't want no trouble with the 'peelers."

Paige opened the door to the cab and pushed Alice into it.

"My grandmother is Lady Ursula Mallory. Take me home," she ordered.

Inside, the two of them collapsed against the leather cushions. They held onto each other and only relaxed when they heard the crack of the cabbie's whip and the clop of the horse's hooves on the cobblestone street. They hugged each other, laughing and crying at the same time, as the cab jerked forward.

14

*I*t took them several minutes to regain their senses. "Horace will be beside himself when he finds us gone!" Alice declared. "I hope he won't take it out on Mary and the boys."

"Don't worry, as soon as we tell Grandmother about this, something will happen. She'll send her lawyer or the police or someone to arrest them." Fury at the Brimleys surged through her. "I'm determined to bring them to justice and free Jeremy, Tom, and Mary. I'm not sure just how to go about it, but Mr. Martengale will know."

Paige felt certain that once Mr. Martengale had heard her story, all the resources at the lawyer's command would be used. Such a crime deserved a harsh punishment. She took a grim satisfaction in that. Maybe Horace and Nettie would get a bitter dose of their own medicine.

As they neared Ashleigh, she leaned forward and looked out the window. They were passing all the places she'd taken for granted—the little cottages, the green grocers, the haberdashery shop, the pub, and finally the small stone church and nearby cemetery. Each familiar landmark made Paige realize how dear the village and everything surrounding it were to her.

The cab's ceiling flap opened, and the cabbie called down, "Where to from here, miss?"

"A little farther up the hill. You can leave us off at the iron gates with the sign MALLORY HALL."

The nearer they got, the more excited Paige became. After all these horrible weeks, she was almost home.

"Alice, we're almost there," she said, reaching over to press Alice's hand, "almost to Mallory Hall."

As soon as the vehicle came to a stop, Paige thrust open the door, got out, then extended her hand to help Alice down. She couldn't help but laugh as she gave the cabbie the gold coin from Alice's tin cup. What a joke on that wretch Horace! How he would have lusted over that sovereign. She took Alice's hand, and they went through the gates and started up the drive.

It was growing dark, but they could see the turreted outline of the roof against the cloudy, gray sky.

"I don't want to risk giving Grandmother a heart attack," Paige told Alice as they approached the house. "We'll go around the back to the tradesmen's entrance. My maid, Flora, may be eating her supper in the servants' hall at this time. I want her to see me first."

Alice just nodded. Her breath was short, and she was limping so badly that Paige stopped to allow her to rest a bit.

"I've also decided I won't tell them right away that I've regained my hearing. I have a feeling I'll learn more if they think I'm still deaf," Paige told Alice.

Paige really didn't know why she'd decided that. Maybe what Alice had overheard from the Brimleys had struck a chord—that her relatives had something to do with her being kidnapped. It still seemed unbelievable, but then . . .

Paige looked up at the house. Lights shone from all the downstairs windows, even from the ones in the drawing and dining rooms. Was her grandmother entertaining? Who could be dining there tonight?

Charles? Back from his tour of duty in Ireland? Paige thought of the song she used to sing to tease him: "Charlie is ma darlin', ma darlin'." She couldn't wait to see him, to see the expression on his face when he saw her.

"Come on, lean on me, " Paige urged Alice. She put her arm around Alice's waist, and they started again toward the house. "Around this way."

Paige led Alice through the kitchen garden to the left of the main entrance. At the door she knocked loudly, and a few moments later a scullery maid she didn't recognize opened it. She realized with some guilt that she didn't know any of the servants very well except Flora, her maid, and Milton, the butler. She had just accepted the fact that hot water was brought upstairs by the undermaids, clean linens were put on her bed, food appeared on the table, floors were scrubbed, and dishes were washed. She now knew what it was like to be treated poorly or ignored. Again she determined she would be different now in the way she treated people.

The girl looked astonished and a little frightened when she saw them. No wonder. They must look a sight in their begging costumes, with their hair tangled, clothes bedraggled, eyes wild. The girl started to slam the door in their faces, probably thinking they were tinkers or beggars or worse. But Paige placed her hand against the door to keep it from closing.

"Wait. Don't be scared. Listen, I must see Flora! Go get her. *At once!*"

The air of authority with which Paige spoke contrasted with her outward appearance and obviously confused the girl.

"F—Flora's helpin' serve tonight," she stammered. "There's company."

Company? Her heart leaped with hope. Maybe she'd guessed correctly. Maybe Charles was here. Why wait while the scullery maid gathered her wits enough to do as she was ordered? Paige pushed her gently to one side and stepped up onto the porch, pulling Alice with her.

"Go fetch Flora. Tell her it's an emergency!"

The girl scurried off, and Paige squeezed Alice's hand.

"It's going to be all right, Alice, just fine. You'll see. I just want to get some idea of what's going on before I make my entrance."

Within three minutes Flora, wearing a black uniform, white ruffled apron, and a cap with its ribbons fluttering, came running out from the kitchen. One look at Paige and she clapped both hands to her mouth, then burst into tears.

"Oh, dear miss," she exclaimed, "is it really you? Oh, mercy me. I canna believe it!"

"Hush, hush, Flora. It's me and I am here. Where did you think I was?"

"Well, miss, in Scotland of course, but—that is, I mean, we thought you was, but oh, you can't hear me anyway—"

"Flora, I *can* hear. I have my hearing back, but you *are not* to tell anyone—not yet."

"Oh, praise be the Lord, miss, it's like a miracle!" Flora clung to her. "The awful news come about your wandering away from the train station," Flora went on, "away from Miss Demetra, and we dinna' know. Oh, our prayers are answered! I've been so worried and—Mr. Martengale and . . ." Her glance went over Paige. "Have you been in a wreck? By the look o' you, miss." Her eyes moved to Alice, who looked even more bedraggled.

"Flora, it's all too much to explain right now. Where is Grandmother?"

"In the dining room, miss. She doesn't always come down anymore, miss. But tonight Mr. Martengale is here. With some news, as much as I can gather from the conversation at the table. But now, miss, you're home, and you *hear* and—"

"It's all right, Flora, I know it's quite a shock. Remember, not a word! I'll tell Grandmother myself when it's time. Who else is here?" she asked, daring to hope it was Charles.

"Mr. Charles, miss. He's returned from Ireland—" She paused as if about to say more, but decided better of it.

"Well then, I'll go on into the dining room and surprise them all." She smiled, imagining just how much of a surprise it would be.

Flora looked concerned. "But, miss, mighten you want to—to tidy up a bit afore—I mean with Mr. Charles bein' here and all?"

Feeling suddenly lighthearted in spite of everything, Paige laughed. "No, Flora, love is blind, isn't it? Don't you think Mr. Charles will be so happy to see me that he won't care how I look?"

Not waiting for an answer, Paige turned to Alice. "Come along, Alice, I want you to meet everyone."

They walked past the pantry through the baize door into the wide central hall of the house. Alice glanced around in awe at the magnificent vaulted ceiling, the polished wood paneling, the parquet floors under fringed Persian rugs in rich colors of red, blue, and gold.

Paige began to feel a mounting tension as they moved toward the dining room. From behind the closed doors she could hear the murmur of voices, the clink of crystal and china. After a split-second hesitation, Paige reached her hand out, opened the doors, and stepped onto the threshold.

15

*T*he dining room was just as Paige remembered it. Lady Ursula, elegantly dressed and coifed, sat regally at the head of the table set with gold-rimmed plates, cut-glass goblets, and silver that gleamed in the candle glow of tall tapers. In the center was an ornate epergne piled with luscious, hothouse fruit.

What a far cry from the bare table in the grim kitchen at the Brimleys'. It seemed impossible that she could have once enjoyed all this luxury, taking it for granted, when so many people lived in degradation and despair. A wave of guilt struck Paige as she thought of Mary, Tom, and Jeremy, who were still in captivity. Her determination to expose the Brimleys strengthened.

At first her appearance at the doorway went unnoticed. She was as invisible as the servants who came and went with barely a word of acknowledgment from the family. The conversation at the table continued until Paige spoke in a loud, clear voice, "Good evening, everyone."

Startled faces turned toward her—the same faces that surrounded her that first morning when she had awakened deaf. Her grandmother, Dr. Grantly, Demetra, and Charles—

and now her grandmother's lawyer, Mr. Martengale. He had not been there then. Why was he here now?

At the sound of Paige's voice, Lady Ursula turned ashen. "Paige!" she gasped. Her beringed hand flew to her breast as if she were having a heart attack.

Demetra half-rose from her chair, staring wide-eyed at Paige, then went to her grandmother's side.

Charles stood up so fast that his chair wobbled and almost fell backward. "Paige!"

He made a movement as if to come toward her, but Dr. Grantly rushed past him, saying, "My dear child! How did you get here? We have been most terribly concerned . . ."

Although Paige was aware of Charles's stunned gaze and the shock Demetra couldn't hide, concern for her grandmother came first. She brushed by the doctor and went to Lady Ursula, who was leaning back in her chair and clutching her throat, her expression one of total shock. Demetra was fanning her with a napkin.

"Where have you been?" Demetra asked in a choked voice. "You look dreadful . . . we have been so worried . . ."

At this point Mr. Martengale took charge. "I suggest we all stay calm and let Miss Mallory tell us her story."

"Remember, everyone," Dr. Grantly intervened, "Paige cannot hear what you're saying. Don't excite her. She looks as if she has been through a terrible ordeal."

Paige took her grandmother's hand and gently held it. "I have so much to tell you all." She glanced around at the faces. Their expressions mirrored a variety of emotions, none of which, strangely, she could easily discern.

Just then Lady Ursula gestured with one shaking hand to Alice, who stood shyly in the doorway. "And who is this?"

Paige beckoned Alice to come to her. When she did, Paige put her arm around her shoulders and drew her close. "Grandmother, there is so much to explain. Alice and I have been through a dreadful experience. It will be hard for you to believe . . ."

Involuntarily her glance shifted to Demetra, whose face had a pinched, wary look. Then Paige's gaze went to Charles, who seemed stunned, unable to move or speak.

Suddenly she felt light-headed. Neither she nor Alice had eaten anything since the pitiful bowl of weak gruel early that morning and their crust of dry bread at noon. Dr. Grantly must have noticed her sudden pallor, because a chair was pulled out for her, and she sat down. "Get some brandy," he ordered the footman standing nearby.

A moment later a glass of brandy was set in front of her, but she shook her head and turned to her grandmother.

"Could Alice and I have something to eat? We've come a long way, and we're very tired and hungry."

"Of course." Lady Ursula imperiously ordered the footman, "Bring some of the lobster bisque immediately."

Paige motioned Alice to sit down on the chair Dr. Grantly had vacated at her entrance. Within minutes, steaming bowls of creamy seafood were placed in front of them, along with fluffy, hot rolls. They had not tasted nourishing food for so long, and they both ate hungrily.

As Paige spooned the thick soup, she made a quick survey of the people gazing at her as though she'd come back from the grave. She noticed a glance pass between Demetra and Charles that both puzzled and disturbed her. Was something going on between them? Something that had occurred in her absence?

She needed time to sort out things, but her head began to throb, and her attention was diverted by Mr. Martengale. Since Alice and Paige had been seated, he had been busily writing something on a pad of paper. As soon as she finished her soup, he handed it to her. She read,

*Miss Mallory, we must have a detailed report of your where-abouts during the past several weeks. Anything you can re-member. Your grandmother received a ransom note from your kidnappers saying they had you in custody and would not re-turn you until an exorbitant sum of money was paid. Your*

*grandmother sent for me, and I in turn hired a private investigator to handle anyone claiming to have any information. Recently this investigator was contacted by someone who said he knew the abductors and where they were keeping you. He offered, for a sizable amount of money, to act as a go-between and secure your freedom. That seemed to me to be a kind of blackmail, taking advantage of a family's distress. But this private investigator is used to these types of petty criminals who are eager to profit from others' dilemmas. So with Lady Ursula's consent, we agreed to his proposition. We had no alternative. Now, you have returned on your own, from all appearances unharmed. We must have a full accounting of what happened to you since your cousin last saw you at the railroad station. All you can remember, the details and descriptions, will do much to secure the kidnappers' arrest.*

Paige finished reading, then looked at him. "You have no idea who this person is?" she asked. "This so-called go-between?"

Mr. Martengale shook his head and wrote on the paper: *As a matter of fact, I shall take great satisfaction in telling that informant that we have no further need of him.* As he gave her his note, the lawyer's face revealed his distaste at having to deal with such a person.

"I will do all I can to help," Paige said after reading his words. "I will need some time to put my thoughts together."

He nodded and wrote: *I quite understand. However, the sooner the better.*

She read from the paper, then glanced at Alice, who looked exhausted. "But first my companion and I need a bath and a good night's sleep."

He looked abject and wrote on his pad: *Of course, quite inconsiderate of me, Miss Mallory. Forgive me.*

Just then Grandmother drew Paige's attention, talking to the others about her as if she weren't even there. "I don't understand. The Sinclair Institute said she never arrived. They never received the cheque for her tuition—"

A numbing weariness began to overtake Paige. She rose from the table. "I'm sorry, Grandmother," she said. "I'm really very tired. I will tell you all I know tomorrow. You must excuse us for now."

"I'll summon Flora," Demetra offered and went to the tapestry bellpull. Flora appeared so quickly that Paige suspected she had been listening to everything at the pantry door.

Demetra spoke as if used to issuing orders. "Take Miss Paige and her—her guest upstairs and bring up hot water for their baths."

Paige glanced at Charles, who still seemed paralyzed by her unexpected arrival. He had not spoken directly to her since she entered the dining room. He was remarkably controlled, not showing any visible sign of emotion, not even relief at her safe homecoming. Unusual behavior for a man whose fiancée had been missing for weeks and perhaps been in harm's way. A man supposedly in love?

Paige reminded herself that Charles had always had difficulty expressing emotion, especially in public. But shouldn't this be an exception? Shouldn't there have been some sort of spontaneous reaction? He should take her in his arms . . . she longed for it. She wanted to make sense of it all. But not now. Tonight she was simply too tired.

She turned to Alice. "Come along."

Finally Charles took a step toward her as they started to leave, but Paige held up her hand, warding him off. "No, wait. I want to get out of these awful clothes. I'll be down after I bathe and change."

He nodded, his face still a mask.

Upstairs, while Alice bathed and Dilys, the young chambermaid, helped wash her hair, Flora filled the huge copper tub in front of the fireplace in Paige's bedroom. She kept up a running monologue while Paige luxuriated in the sudsy, warm water and listened.

"Oh, miss, I've been that worried about ye. Ever since Miss Demetra come back from London alone, I had the strangest feelin'. I thought Miss Demetra was actin' strange herself, but I had no idea, none at all, what had really happened. Then when I found your suitcase with some of your things I put in there meself in the back of her closet—I couldna for the life of me figure it out. The next day first chance I had, I took the liberty of openin' it and saw some of your warmest things, things you'd taken 'specially because the weather in Scotland were still so cold—well, miss, I had the eeriest feelin'—"

"Then Demetra didn't tell Grandmother that she wasn't sure I'd gotten on the train to Scotland?"

Flora pursed her lips. "Not a word, miss. She said afterwards she did not want to upset her ladyship. But then when the letter come from the Institute saying you never arrived, and then the ransom note—well, if you'll excuse me sayin' so . . ." Flora started to say something more, then changed her mind and bit her lower lip before she went on. "There was a terrible scene, indeed! I never seen her ladyship so angry. Both the doctor and Mr. Martengale was sent for and come posthaste. And they're back tonight as luck would have it, talking about what to do before they paid any money to this go-between."

Briefly Paige told Flora what had happened to her that day in the London railroad station and some of what had taken place since then at the Brimleys'. Her recital was punctuated by Flora's horrified gasps, clicking of her tongue, and exclamations. "Oh, my! You poor soul. 'Tis a terrible shame."

"It's all over now. At least for me and Alice. But I've got to do something about those other children. And I will. Do you think Grandmother is strong enough to hear the truth, Flora?"

"Her ladyship is a verra strong lady indeed, miss. She's seen a lot of trouble and trials in her day. I wouldna think this would be too much for her. Besides, she has to know the truth. Remember what the Good Book says, 'You shall know the truth, and the truth shall make you free.'"

Alice, bathed, fed, and with eyes drooping, had been tucked into lavender-fresh sheets in one of the guest rooms when Paige went downstairs.

Paige could tell that everyone had ceased their conversation when she entered the drawing room. Mr. Martengale had departed, and only Dr. Grantly, Charles, Demetra, and her grandmother were there. At her entrance they all seemed like statues in a wax museum exhibit.

Again what Alice had once told her came unwanted into her mind—that all of the inmates at the Brimleys' were the victims of their relatives. Could that be true of *her?*

Suddenly she felt cold, as though surrounded by a malevolence that could only be sensed, never openly acknowledged. Had someone in this room wished her harm? Wanted her out of the way for some reason?

Paige suppressed a shudder. It took all her effort to smile, say, "It's good to be home," and move into the room.

A tray with a plate of sandwiches and a pot of tea was placed on a low table in front of the fireplace, where Dr. Grantly stood as if deep in thought. Grandmother was seated in an armchair and gestured to the one opposite her.

As Paige seated herself, Charles handed her the notebook she recognized as the one they once used to communicate with each other. On it was written in his fine, legible script:

*At first we kept your disappearance from Lady Ursula to avoid causing her undue stress and anxiety. But almost immediately she received word from the Sinclair Institute that you had never arrived. This was followed by a crudely printed ransom note. That's when she called in Mr. Martengale.*

"When did you find out, Charles?" Paige asked.

He wrote: *Demetra contacted me.*

"Do you have the ransom note?" Paige asked.

Charles looked at Demetra, and Demetra at Grandmother, who then opened a drawer in the round piecrust table beside her chair, withdrew a folded piece of paper, and handed it to Paige. Paige unfolded it and read it.

Still holding the note, she looked up at Charles, then at Demetra. "What did you think when you came back with chocolates and magazines and I was gone?" Paige asked, watching Demetra's face and trying to read something—she wasn't sure what—in it.

"I couldn't believe it, Paige," Demetra's words came out in a rush. "The newsstand was crowded, and I had to wait in line. Then when I finally made my purchases, the man was slow giving me change. By the time I ran back to the platform, it was empty. The train had just left, I supposed with you on it—"

"Demetra, write it down," Grandmother's irritated voice interrupted her. "Did you forget Paige is deaf?"

Demetra turned red. "Oh, I'm sorry. Sorry, Paige," she said, all flustered. "Here, Charles, let me have that notepad."

Paige kept silent, waiting. She wanted to be careful, to keep her recovery a secret a little longer. She had to find out more. One of them could slip and say something in her presence that they didn't want her to know. If what Alice had repeated to her of the conversation between the Brimleys was true—that her relatives or someone close to her were somehow involved in her abduction—she had to find out. She turned to Lady Ursula.

"And did you pay the ransom?"

Lady Ursula shook her head and wrote: *No, not at once. I needed advice. Legal advice. I called Martengale. He contacted a private investigator. It was only recently that the person who claimed to know your abductors demanded money to negotiate your release. Before we paid the ransom, you were able to escape.*

Dr. Grantly turned around from the fireplace and spoke to Paige's grandmother. "Lady Ursula, I believe Paige has had enough for tonight. Overexcited, overstimulated, overtired. Can all this not wait until tomorrow?"

Paige's grandmother rubbed her fingers wearily across her forehead and sighed. "Yes, I suppose so. Mr. Martengale will come in the morning and take Paige's deposition, and we shall proceed from there. Of course, now the ransom will never be paid. I wish we had not even given that—" she paused, "that go-between a fee." She shook her head as if to free herself of some distasteful thought.

Lady Ursula wrote on her notepad: *Tomorrow will be time enough to go over all of this. Dr. Grantly thinks you need rest.*

Paige read her grandmother's note and nodded. Maybe it was best to wait until the next day to tell them all her story. Let them wonder how much she knew; it would keep whoever might be guilty in suspense a little longer while she tried to figure out who was telling the truth and who was lying. Paige looked at Charles's handsome face. It revealed nothing. As an officer and a gentleman, personal honor was sacred to him. Would he knowingly have put Paige into that terrible situation? For money? Paige knew Charles, as the youngest son in his family, had nothing monetary other than his army pay. The idea of collecting a sizable ransom might be tempting if he hadn't wanted to marry her after her hearing loss. Paige thrust the thought from her mind as too bizarre. She knew Charles better than that. Didn't she?

Demetra was another story. She didn't know Demetra at all. Had she envied Paige? Paige had continued living in luxury when Demetra and her mother were exiled due to her father's disgrace. And then there was the time Demetra and Charles had spent together when Paige was ill, and the looks she had seen pass between them since her return . . .

Paige tried to rid herself of these thoughts. She must be hallucinating, imagining all sorts of things. Dr. Grantly was right. She felt drained physically and emotionally. She stood up and bent over to kiss her grandmother's powdery cheek. "I'm truly sorry to have put you through all this. It is wonderful to be safely home. Tomorrow we can figure everything out, I'm sure. I seem too tired tonight to think rationally, so I'll say good night to you all."

Paige would have preferred Charles to see her out, but instead Dr. Grantly walked her into the hall and to the staircase. He put a hand on her shoulder and gave her a compassionate look.

All Paige could manage was a nod before she started up the steps. Would tomorrow really be any better? Or would it mean the end of all her preconceived beliefs about her life and the people with whom she was the most closely associated?

aige found Flora waiting for her in her bedroom, turning down the bed and laying out her nightgown and robe.

"Oh, miss, ye do look clear worn out. Let's get ye into bed. I've got the sheets all cozy with the warming pan. Now just let me tuck ye in."

"In a few minutes, Flora. First I need to ask you some questions. I know you know everything that goes on in this house. You must be very honest with me and tell me everything you have heard or observed since I left for Scotland. Anything that seems suspicious."

Flora spoke in a hurried manner, obviously eager for Paige to know everything she had bottled up all these weeks. In the middle of her report they heard a quiet knock at the door.

"May I come in for a moment?" Demetra spoke from the other side.

Flora's eyebrows peaked. When Paige nodded, Flora seemed hesitant, but then reluctantly went to the door and opened it. "Come in, Miss Demetra. But Miss Paige is very tired."

"I understand. I won't stay long." Demetra looked past her to Paige. "I just want her to know how relieved and happy we are to have her home . . ."

Flora looked askance at her, but Paige nodded. Actually, she was glad for the chance to be alone with Demetra, to try to ferret out for herself Demetra's feelings about her disappearance and her return.

"Come in, Demetra," Paige said. "I warn you, though, I might not make much sense. My brain is quite fuzzy."

"I don't intend to keep you awake, Paige." Demetra smiled. "I just wanted to see if you needed anything or wanted anything. Grandmother is quite concerned about you."

Paige feigned a puzzled look.

"Oh, I'm sorry—" Demetra then pulled her notepad out and wrote on it: *Welcome home. We are all so relieved.*

Paige took it and read it, then looked up at Demetra. "Thank you, Demetra."

Flora bustled back over to the bed and patted the satin quilt. "Now, Miss Demetra, Paige must really get into bed and get some sleep, like Dr. Grantly said. Ye ladies can talk tomorrow when Miss Paige is rested."

"You're right, Flora. I'll go now." Demetra went to the door. "Sweet dreams, Paige," she said with a wave, then left.

"Sweet dreams, indeed," Flora grunted. "I dinna know why she didn't let us know right away that ye had disappeared. Waited to telegraph Mr. Charles. Don't ye think that's a wee bit strange?"

Paige did, but how could she discuss this with Flora now? Her brain was too crowded with conflicting ideas. Suddenly she felt overcome with fatigue. Gratefully she crawled into bed and let Flora put the quilt over her, lower the lamp, and go quietly out of the room.

In spite of all the questions clattering for answers in her brain, she did finally go to sleep. She slept soundly until Flora came in with her breakfast tray the next morning and woke her up. The maid informed her that Charles had left shortly after Paige had retired and was staying at the nearby home of friends.

"Did he say what time he would be back today?"

"No, miss, he dinna'," Flora answered, and she might have said more if Paige had pursued the subject.

Paige tried to tell herself it was natural, given his nature, for Charles to be stoic and unemotional about her return. He had to be in a state of shock. Just as soon as they had an opportunity to be alone . . . she did not finish the thought. She couldn't. She knew she had changed since last they were together. Had Charles changed also? Perhaps changed in his feelings about her?

Time for thinking about that later. First things first.

The important thing for her was to cooperate with Mr. Martengale's investigation in every possible way so the Brimleys could be apprehended and arrested. Every day that Mary, Tom, and Jeremy were with them was one too many.

"Has Mr. Martengale come yet, Flora?" Paige asked.

"Yes, miss, and he has a rather strange-looking gentleman with him. Not a real gentleman at all, I'd say, more like a tradesman."

Paige smiled. Servants could be very snobbish, indeed, much more aware of class distinctions than some of the privileged class who were accused of it. The man accompanying the lawyer must be the private investigator hired to deal with the go-between.

Paige made short work of breakfast, and after she dressed she went into the adjoining bedroom to talk to Alice. She told her it was very important that in this meeting she keep up the pretense of being deaf.

"Sign to me as if relaying the information, then I can ask the questions I want answers to. Do you think you can do that? We must see that the Brimleys are caught as soon as possible so that we can free Mary and Jeremy and Tom."

Alice nodded vigorously.

"All right then, let's go downstairs."

In the drawing room they found Dr. Grantly, Paige's grandmother, Mr. Martengale, and the other man Flora had told her about. He rose with the rest of the men as Paige and Alice entered, but seemed somewhat awkward, as though a little awed by the surroundings.

He was of medium height and about forty years of age, with a sharp-featured face and keen eyes. His clothing was neat but not of the best quality. Paige assumed that given the nature of his work, he was used to assessing character and discerning with whom he could deal honestly and of whom he should be suspicious.

Paige quickly explained that Alice would be her interpreter so that the men wouldn't be delayed by having to write everything down.

Everyone seemed relieved at this, and the meeting began. Mr. Martengale opened the discussion. "Mr. Newsome here," he gestured toward the stranger, "has reason to believe that this man, this go-between, who has come forward to volunteer to contact the abductors is known to them by—" he cleared his throat, "—the unfortunate experience of having been incarcerated with Horace Brimley at one time in the same prison."

Grandmother looked alarmed. " A former jail mate? How can such a person be trusted?"

Mr. Martengale exchanged a knowing glance with Mr. Newsome. "My dear Lady Ursula, by the usual method of such types—money, of course. Once promised enough money, he offered to negotiate with Miss Mallory's kidnappers."

Lady Ursula gave a distasteful sniff. "It is too bad we must use his services."

Mr. Newsome shifted forward in his chair as if ready to manifest his expertise in this matter. "Sad to say, yer ladyship, but filthy lucre is the best, and I might even say, the *only* way yer goin' to git any such service from 'em like that one."

Grandmother acknowledged him with a cold stare. He sat back, and Mr. Martengale proceeded.

"After paying the rest of his fee," Martengale inclined his head to Grandmother as if in apology, then continued, "we will arrange a time and place where he is then to meet us with—" here he turned to Paige, "—with Miss Mallory. At which time he will be paid the ransom money agreed upon. As go-between, he has probably arranged to divide it with her captors."

Grandmother gave an impatient gesture.

"I know, Lady Ursula, it is reprehensible, but it is the only way we are going to apprehend the kidnappers."

"How do you propose to do that?" Paige asked after pretending to read Alice's sign language. "Won't he as well as the Brimleys get away scot-free when he realizes I have escaped and he cannot deliver me?"

"No, my dear, not at all. This is where Mr. Newsome's clever plan comes in. I have alerted the district superintendent of police about this matter and have arranged to have them follow our so-called negotiator on his way to make the necessary arrangements with the kidnappers. Thus we can ascertain the location where you were held." He hesitated a few seconds. "Fortunately or unfortunately, whichever way you may look at it, this fellow is already well known to the police. He has a record."

"He may play it cozy," Mr. Newsome interjected, evidently not wanting to be left out of the discussion. "He may just pocket the ransom himself—even if it's half of what they asked—and not lead us to the kidnappers at all. That's wot we gotta watch."

"I want to go with the police," Paige said. "I want to confront the Brimleys myself. We must get Mary and the boys out of their clutches immediately."

"You must be patient, dear. These things take time." Mr. Martengale spoke directly to Alice, and in her enthusiasm, Paige almost forgot to look at Alice for the signs. "We are dealing with criminals, you know. We cannot anticipate what they might do."

"I don't think this fella has a mind to go back to jail," Mr. Newsome volunteered. "He's short of cash, too, and eager to cinch this deal."

"The main point is that he does not yet know that you have escaped and are safely home, that his services are no longer needed, and that we are just using him to locate your captors. That's why we must act swiftly."

"I insist on going," Paige said firmly.

"I don't think that is wise," her grandmother said in a worried tone. "Do you, Mr. Martengale?"

Alice was signing furiously now, trying to keep up.

Paige stood up. "I must, Grandmother. Those villains must be identified. Only Alice and I can do that."

Lady Ursula looked distressed and started to protest, but Mr. Martengale turned to her. "Miss Mallory is right, Lady Ursula. Without her identification of these people, we have only their word to go on. With Alice and Paige no longer there, it is just the three others, who are young and incapable of defending themselves. There is no positive evidence that any of them have been mistreated, without Paige's testimony. Our understanding is that the children other than Miss Mallory were put into the Brimleys' custody on the assumption that they would be well cared for. Since we only have Miss Mallory's word as to the treatment the others also received, it is necessary to have her there as a witness." He paused and turned to Dr. Grantly. "We also need the doctor's statement that she is deaf and was made to beg on the streets."

Grandmother shuddered.

"So it is decided then." Mr. Martengale glanced around the room for everyone's approval of the plan.

Grandmother agreed on the condition that Flora would accompany Alice and Paige in the carriage, which would remain behind the police following the go-between.

Alice and Paige hurried upstairs to alert Flora and to find warm cloaks and hats while the carriage was brought around. They first went to Mr. Martengale's office, where they would wait until Mr. Newsome informed them that the rest of the go-between's money had been paid to the man. Then, if the plan worked, they would follow the go-between to the kidnappers' house.

It was an overcast day, and Paige found herself shivering both from the penetrating fog as well as from nerves. To think that at last the Brimleys were about to be arrested, and justice done, was exciting. Paige held Alice's hand, squeezing it tightly.

Moments later, Mr. Martengale dispensed instructions and saw the girls out to the carriage parked outside his office, where they would remain until Mr. Newsome came out with the go-between. He would engage him in some kind of last-minute conversation, which would signal the police hidden nearby.

It seemed an eternity as they waited now, peering discreetly out of the carriage window, watching the door of the building. Finally two men emerged and came down the steps in full view.

Suddenly Flora clutched Paige's arm. "Oh, my land, miss!" Flora gasped as her fingers dug through the wool of Paige's coat sleeve. "It *can't* be! But it *is!*"

"It's *what,* Flora? It's who?"

"Oh, miss, it's Basil Colfax!"

emetra's father? Are you sure?"

"Positive, miss," Flora said breathlessly. "I saw him often before it happened—the embezzlement and all. There was terrible scenes, shoutin' and such. Miss Helena weepin' and carryin' on somethin' awful. I come face-to-face with Basil Colfax many times. Fierce he was, and bleary-eyed with drink." Flora shuddered. "Oh yes, miss, I'd never forget him. That's Basil Colfax for sure."

This information left Paige shaking. How did it all fit in with her abduction? Did Demetra know? Was she the relative who had arranged it all, as Alice had suggested? Paige could hardly believe it. She knew Demetra could be manipulative for her own reasons. But to be part of a criminal conspiracy?

Paige scarcely had a moment to absorb this new information when the carriage door opened and Mr. Martengale got in, wearing a serious expression. He patted his waistcoat, then the pockets of his jacket, and seemed frustrated. He must have forgotten his notepad and was wondering now how to communicate with her. He was about to say something to Alice, when Paige decided to end her charade.

She leaned forward. "I can hear, Mr. Martengale. I thought it best not to reveal this before, to gather more evidence, but . . ." She quickly told him of the blow Horace had inflicted on her that brought back her hearing.

Mr. Martengale looked shocked, then angry. "If you can testify to that and have Dr. Grantly confirm your deafness before you were abducted, we can build an even stronger case against him."

"Please tell me what has transpired," begged Paige.

"It seems that the two blind boys' grandparents are coming to get them today to take them to the dock, where they will meet their parents' ship. The go-between did not want to approach the house until tomorrow, when the Brimleys will not have company and he can work a deal."

"He still doesn't know Alice and I have escaped?"

"He'll find out soon enough," Mr. Martengale said grimly. "That's when the police will move in and arrest them."

"Mr. Martengale, my maid, Flora, has brought something else to my attention. It may be that this go-between your investigator is using is known to my family. In fact, I believe he may be my estranged stepuncle."

"Surely not, Miss Mallory! This is extraordinary! What do you mean?"

"Did you get his name from Mr. Newsome?"

"In passing," the lawyer replied, "a Mr. Jones. Of course, I imagine he is working under an assumed name. I knew he was a questionable character who was after money, but as he was also helping us find you, I gave him little thought, preferring to let Mr. Newsome handle him."

"I'm sure it's Basil Colfax!" Flora exclaimed. "I saw him! Indeed, I'm sure o' it. He's Miss Demetra's father," she told the astounded lawyer.

"And he is my stepuncle," Paige said, "though I've not seen him since I was a child. I did not recognize him."

"Indeed!" Mr. Martengale exclaimed again. "This complicates matters a great deal. We thought our go-between was a minor party in this scheme, and these Brimleys you described were the criminal perpetrators. But if this is true, it alters everything. Miss Mallory, you say you haven't seen him since you were young. What reason would he have to hold a grudge against you or be involved in such criminal actions?"

"There was a family scandal, Mr. Martengale—perhaps Grandmother informed you of it?"

"It was before my time," Mr. Martengale replied. "When I was retained by your grandmother, she made it clear that I should serve her in legal and monetary matters only. Her former lawyer, who was retiring, informed me that she was a proud and private woman who would not tolerate personal inquiries beyond those necessary for business. I heard intimations of family difficulties, but thought it best to let the past alone. Do go on . . ."

"My stepuncle was accused of not only squandering family money but embezzling it for himself from the estate to pay his debts. My grandmother would neither absolve him nor pay his creditors, so he went to jail. My Aunt Helena and Demetra were forced to leave Mallory Hall, ashamed and penniless. It was only recently, since my engagement, that Demetra and I have been reunited."

"But—does this mean she too may be involved?" he inquired. "I am sorry, but we must explore the possibilities," he apologized as he saw tears spring into Paige's eyes at this suggestion.

"I . . . I don't know," Paige stammered. "Demetra is so cold toward me . . . I can't blame her. She grew up in dire circumstances, while I remained comfortably at Mallory Hall. I feel she has begrudged it, but to think of her involved in this—I don't know . . ." she finished lamely.

"Of course not, Miss Mallory, you've been through a great deal. But even so, your hardships have not turned you criminal. Let us hope your cousin is innocent, but if not, the hardship she has borne because of her father is no excuse for criminal action. Whatever the case, we will make sense of this and see justice done," Mr. Martengale promised, handing Paige his handkerchief along with his sympathy.

"Thank you," Paige said, wiping her eyes and sitting up with new resolve. She knew Mr. Martengale was right—no amount of personal hardship could be excuse enough to expose a disabled person to the likes of Horace and Nettie Brimley. Even if her relatives were involved in all of this, rescuing Mary, the boys, and others like them was far more important to her now than family pride.

"What do we do next?" she asked Mr. Martengale.

"I suspect that if your stepuncle is the culprit behind all you have suffered, then the ransom note was actually from him," the lawyer surmised. "No doubt the amount he offered the Brimleys was far less than the amount he planned to keep for himself. Perhaps he arranged a separate deal with the Brimleys to provide a 'safe' hiding place for you until your grandmother could supply the ransom money for your return. Then he posed as a go-between, pretending to approach Mr. Newsome as someone with information on the whereabouts of the 'real' kidnappers.

"It's a devious twist, planning to frame the Brimleys as the criminals if it came to that, when they may have simply been the malicious underlings in his crime," the lawyer continued. "Put bluntly, they've been doing his dirty work so he could collect the ransom. I propose we continue with our original plan of letting him lead us to the Brimleys' location tomorrow. This way we can catch more than two birds with one stone. We don't know what amount he is planning to pay the Brimleys, but I wager he is planning to keep most of the ransom he expects to get by delivering you, Miss Mallory."

"And of course I won't be at the Brimleys' when he gets there. That is, until we follow the police in and I confront them myself."

"You are still determined to do that? It's risky and could be dangerous. Horace Brimley has a reputation for violence."

"I don't need to be told *that*, Mr. Martengale."

"So then we wait. The go-between will signal us here to-morrow, letting us know when we can head toward the Brim-leys' house where you were held." Mr. Martengale opened his briefcase and brought out a piece of paper, which he handed to Paige. "I'm afraid there's more. We have discovered the Brimleys' operation is not an isolated case. It seems many such unscrupulous havens are offered to families. Not all of them are as bad as what you've been subjected to, but here—read it for yourself. This ad appears in many newspapers."

Paige took the copy of the advertisement.

WE CARE when you cannot. If you want a safe place to board your blind, deaf, or crippled relative, look no further. We offer a homelike, caring residence—year-round, holidays included. Reasonable fees, confidential.

The hypocrisy of it sickened Paige. She thought of the con-ditions they had lived in and the treatment they had received at the hands of the Brimleys. Punishment could not come soon enough for the kind of people who preyed on the des-perate and helpless.

"Under the circumstances, I believe having Dr. Grantly along tomorrow might be a good thing as well. I will send word for him to meet us at my office now, if you can stay to see him."

In the lawyer's office, Dr. Grantly stroked his mustache and adjusted his wire-rimmed glasses as he listened intently to Paige's story. The doubt and incredulity in his eyes began to change as she told him about the savage blow that had somehow restored her hearing.

"Of course, there is such a thing as spontaneous healing. I hoped your loss of hearing might gradually come back, but I never imagined it would be in this brutal manner," Dr. Grantly said.

The doctor was visibly upset by her revelations and agreed to accompany them to the Brimleys' the next day. They would wait for Mr. Newsome to tell them that the "informant" Paige now knew as Basil Colfax was ready to go there and "rescue" her for ransom.

When the girls got back to Mallory Hall, it was late in the afternoon. Grandmother's maid told them that Lady Ursula was napping, so Paige asked that tea for herself and Alice be brought up to her room.

Once in her room, Paige questioned Flora closely about her identification of Basil Colfax, but the maid insisted it was him.

"The strange part is no one has seen or heard of him since he was taken away. His prison sentence was quite a long one, though I don't remember the exact amount of time he was to serve. Miss Helena was never very close to her stepmother, your grandmother. His trial was in all the papers. Terrible humiliatin' for Lady Ursula to have the family name dragged through the mud like that. Right after the trial Miss Helena and Demetra, who was just about ten at the time, left here."

The three of them went over the surprising events of the day, exchanging views and impressions of all that had happened.

"I can't wait to see Horace's face when he sees us!" exclaimed Alice. "Oh, Paige, you are so brave. If it wasn't for you, I'd still be in their clutches." Her face puckered. "Poor Mary is still there."

"Not for long, and at least Jeremy and Tom are safely out of there with their grandparents by now."

"Do you think the boys will tell them about what the Brimleys are really like?"

"I don't know, but I intend to contact their families and Mary's sisters too. If there is a trial, we all may need to testify. Dr. Grantly has promised to verify my deafness and recovery."

Suddenly Paige became aware of a slight sound outside her bedroom door—the scuttle of a mouse, a skirt brushing by, a footstep?

She put her finger on her mouth, warning the other two to stop talking, then she tiptoed over to the door and stood listening. She placed her hand on the knob, ready to yank it open and disclose a possible eavesdropper. She turned it quickly and opened the door.

There was no one there. Maybe she was mistaken. Then, down the hall, she heard a door quietly close.

18

The next morning, Paige was wide awake at dawn. Nervous about the surprise visit to the Brimleys' and the confrontation that would follow, she could not go back to sleep. It was too early for Flora to come with her breakfast tray. Paige got out of bed and went to the window, drawing aside the draperies.

Fog hung like a gray veil, and she looked out into it, contemplating the scene that would take place later that day. But then, through the heavy mist, she saw two figures at the gate at the end of the driveway. Who were they? And what were they doing there at this hour? Possibly one of the maids and her boyfriend, meeting before they had to report for work or returning from a rendezvous?

Grandmother had strict rules about her female servants having "followers," and the housekeeper, Mrs. Barkley, vigilantly made sure that these rules were obeyed. Paige started to turn away when what looked like an altercation began between the two figures. The man was gesturing wildly. The woman started to leave, but he grabbed her arm. She pulled away from him, and he flung her off and stalked away. She began to run after him and was swallowed up in the enveloping fog.

A lovers' quarrel? Possibly. But Paige had no time to dwell on this curious scene. She had more urgent things on her mind.

It would soon be time to get ready for the trip to the Brimleys' and the confrontation with her captors. She both looked forward to it and dreaded it.

An hour later, Paige, Alice, and Flora slipped quietly out of the house and into the waiting carriage. As they neared Mr. Martengale's office, where Mr. Newsome and the police would meet them, Paige reached for Alice's hand. Only they really knew what they would face when confronting the Brimleys.

Mr. Newsome, Mr. Martengale, and Dr. Grantly were outside conferring with the police when Paige's carriage arrived. Mr. Newsome was visibly upset.

"I tell you, there's no possible way Colfax could've found out about Miss Mallory's escape," he blustered. "But I tailed him last night to make sure we didn't lose him, and the only place he goes to was his own. First thing this mornin' he heads o'er to Mallory Hall. I watched him close, suspectin' the worst and 'fraid for Miss Mallory's safety. He meets with another girl out by the gate, one o' them purty, young maids or some such, then he's gone—skips town and don't look back. She musta told him the news. It's the only way he coulda knowed the game's up."

"Well, one bird's flown the coop," a burly police sergeant said, "but that don't mean we can't catch the other two in our net. I had me boys do some roustin' about after Mr. Newsome here let us in on Miss Mallory's descriptions of her ordeal. Sure enough, one knew this 'Orace Brimley character from the old days. Brimley landed himself in jail back then, but once he got out, he seemed to settle himself down with his missez nice and quietlike.

"Keepin' an eye on the pubs hereabouts, my officer knew where this Brimley loads himself up. He loads up more than drink too—he seen him loading two boys that fit Miss Mallory's description of the blind ones into a wagon a couple days back, and he tailed it. We got Brimley's house pinned down, and we have a warrant when you give the word."

"Magnificent!" Mr. Martengale beamed.

Mr. Newsome looked vastly relieved. "That's investigatin' at its best!" he told the sergeant. "Let's have a go, then."

Mr. Martengale, with the private investigator and the police sergeant, got into the first carriage, which led the way. The police van followed at a distance. After they passed the railroad station, they went only a few more miles before they stopped in front of a row of perfectly ordinary looking houses. Paige was astonished. Horace must have taken a circuitous route to disorient them. So this was how they had deceived the unsuspecting families of the disabled. For all appearances, this was a decent, middle-class neighborhood. The Brimleys' neighbors surely never suspected the nefarious business in which the couple was engaged.

Mr. Martengale, Mr. Newsome, and the sergeant got out and walked to an unobtrusive-looking vehicle resembling some kind of delivery truck—a police transport used for such raids. Mr. Martengale had explained their plan to Paige and Alice, so they had some idea what to expect. The sergeant conferred for a few minutes with a plainclothes detective and two policemen. Then Mr. Martengale came over to Paige's carriage, opened the door, and leaned his head inside.

"The police will follow Newsome and stay hidden until he knocks on the door and gains admittance, then they will be right behind him, brandishing a search warrant. We will follow closely and step into the house. Are you ladies ready? Be prepared for anything. We don't know exactly what will happen."

Paige felt her heart banging against her ribs. This was the moment of truth—the moment of confrontation with her captors. She whispered a prayer for strength, and, holding

Alice's hand, got out of the carriage and followed Mr. Martengale across the street.

Mr. Newsome knocked firmly on the door of the house. They waited, and Paige held her breath. They heard the rattle of a chain lock being removed, the twisting sound of another lock, and then the door opened a few inches.

"Yeah, what do you want?"

It was still early. Was Nettie alone? Horace might not have yet returned from delivering his victims to their begging posts. Then Paige remembered that Tom and Jeremy had been collected by their grandparents, and only little Mary remained there.

"We have a search warrant for this house," Mr. Newsome said firmly.

"Whatcha mean?"

"That means we have authority to come into this house. Search it."

"'Orace!" Nettie screamed, but before she could slam the door shut, Newsome signaled the policemen, and they moved inside.

Mr. Martengale stepped in behind the police, and the girls quickly followed.

They could hear heavy footsteps coming down the hall, and a moment later Horace appeared, sliding his suspenders up over his shoulders.

"What's all the racket about?" Horace grumbled, then stopped in his tracks and swore.

"Police business," one of the officers said. "You and your wife are under arrest. We have a search warrant."

The two policemen came forward to surround him. Nettie backed up against the wall. Her flabby face crumpled, and her eyes widened in fear.

"I told you it weren't a good idea to get mixed up with that fella—" she whined.

"Shut your face," snarled Horace. He let out a string of curses and took a few steps backward.

*140*

The policemen moved steadily forward, forcing the Brimleys down the hall. Backed into the kitchen, Horace stumbled against the table. Nettie, her shoulders scrunched, was visibly quivering.

Mr. Martengale then stepped to the front.

"We have reason to believe you are responsible for the disappearance and outrageous treatment of persons unable to speak for themselves, kept here against their will. And furthermore, you have sent a note demanding ransom for the return of a Miss Paige Mallory, abducted from Victoria Station a month ago."

Horace's mouth fell open. "Nuthin' o' the kind," he blubbered. "Where'd yer git that? Yer can't prove nuthin'. Dunno wot yer talkin' about."

"Oh no?" Mr. Martengale replied calmly. He turned to Paige and Alice, beckoning them to come closer. "We have witnesses who will testify to the contrary."

"You ain't got any proof on me. It were this other fella. He thought up the whole thing, wrote the note—we were doin' all right until—" Horace stopped as Paige stepped from behind Mr. Martengale and faced him. The expression on Horace's face changed from disbelief to fury, his color from red to purple. "Dunno wot yer talkin' 'bout. I never seen these two."

"You deny that you and your wife keep blind, deaf, and otherwise unfortunate persons in horrible conditions, exploiting them for your own financial gain by having them pose as beggars while you receive payments from their families, who believe you are rendering them good care?"

"I deny everythin'," Horace muttered, but his eyes were those of a trapped animal.

"You deny you inflicted bodily harm on this young lady?" Mr. Martengale put his hand on Paige's arm, while she stared at Horace.

"Never seen her, I ain't."

*141*

"You deny that you conspired to kidnap her, bring her here, and collect a huge amount of money from her grandmother through a co-conspirator?"

Nettie was clutching her apron to her mouth, darting frightened looks around the room as if seeking a means of escape.

"'Orace, tell 'im about Colfax," she blurted. "Don't let 'im get away scot-free."

At the mention of that name, Flora pinched Paige's arm.

Horace glanced briefly at Nettie, then, "That's right. It were none of our idea."

Just then they heard running footsteps down the hall. A minute later Mary, looking like a pale little wraith in bare feet and a nightgown miles too large for her, stood in the doorway.

*Alice! Paige! Oh, I'm so glad to see you!* Mary signed with trembling fingers.

They both ran over to her, embracing her tiny body. She felt like skin and bones. She started coughing, a racking, hard cough. She had apparently not fully recovered from the drenching she had received in the rain. And who knew what kind of indifferent care she had been receiving from Nettie?

Horace took advantage of the diversion to make a break for it, moving quickly and smoothly toward the kitchen door leading outside. Paige, seeing him move, whirled around and stuck out her foot, tripping him and landing him flat on the floor.

"Good work, Miss Mallory!" Mr. Newsome declared, giving Paige an admiring glance.

The two policemen were on Horace in a moment, pulling his hands behind his back as he lay prone and handcuffing him. At almost the same time, the plainclothes detective entered the kitchen.

"Horace Brimley, you are under arrest for kidnapping, extortion, and inflicting bodily harm on persons who will be swearing out these charges." To the policemen, he ordered, "Take him away."

Nettie stood there blubbering into her apron, while Flora wrapped her shawl around Mary.

"She's to come with us," Paige said to Mr. Martengale and Alice. "Tell her she'll stay at Mallory Hall until I can get in touch with her sisters."

When Alice signed this to Mary, tears began to roll down Mary's thin cheeks, and her smile was tremulous.

The policemen shoved Horace out the door, while Horace shouted obscenities. "It's Colfax you want. He planned the whole thing. I'd never have thought of it. People come to us. I don't go snatchin' anyone off the street."

Flora and Paige looked at each other. If Demetra's father were involved in this dastardly scheme, how much did Demetra herself know?

*P*aige sent Mary home to Mallory Hall with Flora to be fed, put in a warm bed, comforted, and coddled. Alice and Paige, accompanied by Mr. Martengale, went to the police station and signed papers corroborating each other's account of the Brimleys' operation.

The sergeant told Paige that she would also need a statement from her physician about her deafness. Then it could be determined that Horace's blow was strong enough to cause a physical reaction that restored her hearing. She assured him she would get such a statement from Dr. Grantly.

By the time Paige and Alice returned to Mallory Hall, they were both exhausted. After assuring herself that Mary was cozily ensconced in the small room adjoining Alice's, Paige told Flora to ask Cook to send up a hearty tea for the two girls. Alice would get all the information about Mary's sisters in order to contact them.

Paige went to her own room then, feeling emotionally and physically drained. Never in her wildest dreams could she have imagined a day like today. She had led such a sheltered life, she hadn't even known that people as corrupt as the Brimleys or Basil Colfax existed. What would Grandmother think when the truth was known? And Demetra? How would they deal with her?

As if thoughts of her cousin had summoned her, Flora appeared then with the tea tray and a message.

"I met Miss Demetra as I come upstairs, miss. She'd like to have a word with ye." Flora's raised eyebrows spoke volumes.

"Certainly, Flora, tell her to come in."

Flora left the room, and a moment later Demetra entered.

"I just wanted to say how relieved I am that your ordeal is over," Demetra began. "I was worried sick when you disappeared."

Had she forgotten Paige could not hear?

Paige bit her tongue, wanting to challenge that statement in light of what she knew about Demetra's father's involvement in her kidnapping.

"When I came back from the station newsstand," she went on, "and you were gone, I was completely upset."

Paige just looked at her.

"Oh, I—" Demetra started to reach for the notepad on Paige's desk.

"Were you, Demetra?" Paige's tone was noncommittal. The charade was over. She wanted to confront Demetra, but didn't know exactly what to say. How would Demetra explain her part in all this? "*Were* you completely upset?" Paige challenged.

Startled now, or pretending to be, Demetra took a step back. "You can *hear!*" she gasped, then, in an accusing tone, "You *can* hear, can't you, Paige?"

"Yes, Demetra, the result of being boxed on my ears and thrown down a steep, wooden staircase."

Demetra went sickly pale. "Does Charles know?"

"Not yet."

"And Grandmother?"

"I'll tell them both tomorrow."

"I didn't know what to do, Paige," Demetra's words came in a rush. "I asked passersby if they had seen you. I described your appearance, but you had vanished into thin air. I didn't know who to turn to. That's when I telegraphed Charles. I didn't know what else to do. I was afraid Grandmother might have a heart attack. That's why I kept it from her. I didn't know if you had disappeared on your own, if you had planned to run away, if you were on the train, or what."

Paige looked at her incredulously. "You never suspected I might have been kidnapped, Demetra, bound and gagged and abducted?"

"How could I know?"

"You knew who was behind all this," Paige said coldly. "You might have gone straight to the police, Demetra."

"The police?"

"Indeed. As I have done."

Demetra's eyes widened with fear.

"I was kept in a place where a criminal operation is conducted. Fraud. A front, supposedly to care for the disabled. It was used as a place of confinement for *me*. Now I've exposed it. Anyone involved will be brought to justice."

Demetra looked genuinely shocked. "I had no idea—"

Paige raised her eyebrows. "No?"

Demetra's eyes narrowed. "Are you planning to implicate me in this?"

Paige said quietly, "He is *your* father."

Demetra bit her lower lip, struggling for composure.

"It wasn't my fault! It wasn't my idea! It would never have occurred to me to do anything like this. At first, I didn't know what he was going to do. Not the whole plan. He needed money; he wanted revenge. Who could blame him? He spent ten years in prison for something Grandmother could have easily fixed—the amount of money was so small. Just to pay off some gambling debts. Terrible people were pressuring him. He intended to pay it back. That's what he always told us. Mother and me . . . He just didn't have time to—" She took a long, shaky breath. "When he heard you were deaf and might not recover . . . The night of the Sinclair lecture, he approached me. He wanted to know what you were going to do."

*147*

Paige realized Basil Colfax must've been the man who had brought their carriage around. The way he had looked at her that night—Paige shuddered.

Demetra continued. "It sounded simple. And after Grandmother gave permission for you to go to Scotland, he decided—it was only to be a short time they held you. I had no idea what it was going to be like for you! He knew Horace because they were in prison together. Horace had told him about the home he and his wife had for cripples and the like. It sounded nothing like you say it was. Believe me, Paige, I never guessed. My father took me to see the place, the Brimleys' house. It looked fine, comfortable. I didn't know about anything else. He met me at the railroad station right before you were to leave for Scotland. He took the tuition money and your travel expenses as a downpayment to the Brimleys to keep you until Grandmother paid the ransom. Paige, I didn't know . . ." Her voice broke. "He's my father. How could I refuse?"

Paige didn't know what to say. "Was he with you at the gate yesterday morning?" she asked.

"Yes, I had to get word to him that you were back, so he wouldn't go to the Brimleys' and be arrested along with them. He was furious that you had escaped before he could collect the rest of the ransom money for your return. It would kill him to have to go back to prison." Then her demeanor changed and her expression hardened. "How could *you* possibly understand? You've always had everything given to you on a silver platter. You don't know what it is to be poor, disgraced, your very name an indictment. No, *you've* only cared for yourself! Even Charles is aware of that." Then, as if she had said too much, Demetra started toward the door. There she turned back. "Do what you want, Paige. Turn me over to the police, whatever. I don't care anymore."

With that she went out the door, letting it slam behind her.

Paige sat completely still. Demetra's actions were inexcusable, but Paige had to admit her accusations had some truth in them. Paige had experienced a rude awakening from self-centered ignorance during her captivity. But some good must come out of all this misery. Paige was determined to carry through her intention to expose such fraud as the Brimleys represented, to do something to make life better for the unfortunate and disabled such as she herself had been for a brief time. She wasn't sure what to do about Demetra, but she would never forget what had happened to her, and she must now use that experience to help others.

## 20

hat night Paige slept fitfully, and the next morning she awakened to Flora's worried face bending over her. Sensing something was wrong, Paige sat up. "What is it, Flora?"

"Oh, miss, I took Miss Demetra her tea, but—she's gone, miss. Her bed hasn't been slept in, her wardrobe is emptied, not a hairpin nor hanky anywhere."

Paige threw back the covers.

Gone? Demetra gone? Paige reached for her robe and followed Flora down the hall to the room Demetra had occupied.

It was in complete disarray—a contrast to Demetra's usual neatness. Dresser drawers were half open, the wardrobe doors ajar, things dropped in a trail on the floor as if discarded in her flight. The dressing table was swept clean of toiletries. Demetra had emptied it of any personal items. She had obviously left in great haste. Paige glanced around the room, and her eyes fell on the desk, its drawers hanging open. Paige went over and pulled open the drawers farther. In the back of one she saw a bunch of letters Demetra had evidently overlooked.

Paige picked up the letters and rifled through them. They were from Demetra's mother, Helena Colfax. At random Paige read snatches of Helena's letters. In one she had written, *From what you tell me, the wedding is now postponed due to Paige's unexpected illness. May I remind you that it is an "ill wind that blows no good." This may be the very opportunity you need to ingratiate yourself with Lady Ursula, who is very selfish and likes to be waited upon, agreed with, and freed from all the petty annoyances of life. If Paige's illness is as serious as the doctors say, you should have plenty of time to do this.*

Another letter with a later date: *Paige deaf? I suggest you resign your position as governess to Lady Hadley's children at once and settle at Mallory Hall to make yourself indispensable to your grandmother.*

The next one was full of motherly instructions: *This is a time of unprecedented opportunity. Your grandmother is in the social position to present you to eligible young men who would make excellent marriage prospects. What about Paige's young man? Surely he does not want to be saddled with a deaf wife?*

It was in the next letter that Paige received written proof of the plot involving Demetra as well as her parents: *Your father will meet you at the lecture hall where Alistair Sinclair will be speaking. He will give you instructions then regarding what you are to do.*

Paige drew in a long breath. The man who had brought their carriage around in the rain after Sinclair's lecture had to have been Basil Colfax. She remembered how he had looked her directly in the face as if memorizing it. Of course, he had not seen her since she was a child. He would have to know how to describe her to Nettie Brimley so she would know her at the train station.

Paige stood there with the incriminating letters in her hand. It would be an unpleasant piece of work to accuse her own cousin of conspiring with criminals. Demetra's excuse that her father forced her into compliance would hardly stand up in court. No matter that her father had been a thief, an embezzler. Whatever the case, she was gone. And Paige was not about to pursue her. It wasn't worth it just to get her testimony against the Brimleys. They had all the evidence they needed to get a conviction, Paige was sure of it. Alice, Mary, Tom, and Jeremy would all sign depositions. It would certainly be enough. Then and there, she decided to burn the letters.

Afterwards Paige felt shaky and sick. At Flora's insistence she ate some toast and drank some tea, then she put on warm clothes and walked down to the stables to see her horses for the first time in weeks. She needed fresh air to clear her head and time to absorb the events of the last few days.

The head groom greeted her cheerfully and expressed his pleasure on her recovery. She stroked the velvety nose of her favorite mare, Mayling, who whinnied in recognition. She fed her and Templar, her next favorite mount, the sugar lumps she'd brought with her.

"I shall start riding again soon," she told the groom. While she was deaf, Dr. Grantly had forbidden it due to her lack of equilibrium. "Who has been exercising them all this time?" she asked.

"Miss Demetra and Lieutenant Bennett, when he's here, miss."

Paige felt a spurt of anger. Demetra taking her place on her horse, riding out with Charles, seemed an especially cruel affront.

She left the stables and took the long way back to the house through the winter gardens. The invigorating air had indeed swept the cobwebs from her brain, and she could think more clearly than before. At the top of the driveway she stopped suddenly and looked down at the road, remembering the scene she had witnessed in the misty dawn. Two figures, a man and a woman, in heated discussion. Foiled in his plan to collect the ransom, Basil Colfax must have angrily chastised his daughter. And now Demetra was gone.

Deep in thought, she resumed her walk, quickening her pace. She would have to consult with Mr. Martengale to tell him all that she had learned from Demetra's outburst the night before, as well as what she'd observed that morning at the gate.

She went inside and was startled to see Charles's military cape, hat, and gloves on the chair in the front hall.

At the sound of her entrance, he appeared at the door of the drawing room. He looked anxious. "Paige, I've been waiting for you. We must talk." He glanced over his shoulder, as if at any minute they might be interrupted. "Let's go into the conservatory where we can speak privately."

That struck her as a singularly significant place. The conservatory had been the setting for some of their most intimate moments—their first kiss, their first declaration of love, his proposal, her acceptance.

They walked into the glassed room, where the pale morning sun shone through the panes onto the various exotic plants. Paige was conscious of the heavy fragrance of lilies but was unprepared for the feelings of nostalgia the scent brought her: the perfume worn by her elusive mother, her father's funeral when she was a very little girl, and lastly, her own debut ball when Charles had waltzed her into this fairyland of flowers.

When she had first returned she had longed for Charles to take her in his arms, hold her close, and tell her how relieved and happy he was to have her back. Now she felt nothing but distance between them.

Charles began to pace and refused to look directly at her. Paige noticed that he had no notebook in which to write his communications to her.

"You know I can hear?"

Charles nodded. "Yes, Demetra told me."

"Demetra?"

"Yes, at the village train station early this morning. I was arriving on the London train, and she was leaving. We only had a few minutes to talk. She was very distraught."

"Did she tell you everything?"

"Everything?"

"About her father? That he was the mastermind behind my kidnapping?"

Charles frowned and shook his head. "No, perhaps there wasn't time. I had come to speak to you on a different matter altogether. Now that you are no longer deaf, it makes what I have to say easier." His handsome face flushed. Hands clasped behind his back, Charles began to pace again.

"Tell me, then," Paige said carefully and took a deep breath. Deep in her heart she knew what he had come to say. Even in the first weeks of her recovery, she had seen his discomfort with the sickroom and his aversion to conducting their conversations in writing. And she had to admit that her sensitivity to being excluded and her outbursts of temper had contributed to the unspoken estrangement her deafness had caused between them.

"I'm very glad for you, that you've regained your hearing even though you went through a horrible experience to do so." He paused.

"But that is not what you want to talk about, is it, Charles?"

"Well, of course, in a way it is," he hesitated, flustered. "In another way it isn't. I want to talk about the future."

"The future," Paige repeated. "Yes, that is a good place to start, I suppose."

"You know I wanted you to go to the Sinclair Institute. Encouraged you—"

"Because it might make me more suitable, more acceptable as your wife?"

Charles looked offended. "No. I felt it would help you live better with your hearing loss."

Despite this protest, slowly the realization came to Paige that his love for her had not survived—not her illness, not her deafness, not her mysterious disappearance. Deep down she had known it all along. Charles had fallen in love with her as a lively, physically strong young woman. But she had never suspected that a hint of her fortune might have sped up his proposal.

Before she lost her hearing, Paige had been everything he could have hoped for in a future wife, an asset to his career. Now she saw that certainly her wealth, over which he would have some control when they married, might have been an important factor.

"I knew it would help you—"

"I think what you actually wanted," Paige interrupted, "was for things to be the same as when we became engaged, before I was ill, before we had this or any other problems."

Charles seemed at a loss for words. He must have been more prepared for an emotional scene. He hadn't anticipated that Paige would accept things so coolly.

"I've just come to see that we are, after all, maybe not suited for each other, Paige."

At his halting words, Paige felt a coldness sweep over her, perhaps because of a deeply remembered pain of other losses. And yet at the same time she felt a kind of freedom, a letting go of something she had clung to because there had been nothing, no one else.

She took a breath and found her voice.

"It's all right, Charles. Strangely enough, it doesn't surprise me. I have changed. My deafness and what happened to me as a result has done that." She drew a long breath. "I release you from our engagement. Isn't that what you want?"

He looked relieved. "What will you do?"

Paige almost laughed. Charles was so full of self-importance that he naively assumed that without him she would be bereft.

"I have plans you probably wouldn't approve of, people to see, things to do that are personal. I have an obligation, a duty—you understand duty, Charles, don't you? A duty to right a terrible wrong that has been perpetrated on innocent, helpless victims, mostly children. I have to do this. It comes before everything else."

*156*

Charles shifted from one foot to the other. "There is one thing more, Paige. Something I didn't tell you—couldn't tell you, before . . . While I've been stationed in Ireland I've become very fond of my commanding officer's daughter—and well," he paused, embarrassed, "you see, it was my mother's . . . the ring."

"Of course."

So there *was* someone else, perhaps had been for months. Even as she lay in the Brimleys' cellar, thinking of him.

"Wait here, I'll get it."

Once upstairs, Paige removed the box containing the engagement ring from the drawer where she'd put it before her ill-fated trip to London. Strangely enough, only the night before, she'd taken it out and looked at it a long time. Paige felt a tiny pang of regret. It was the symbol of another life, of dreams never fulfilled, of a carefree time that was now over. But like Charles, the ring had never fit quite right anyway. She saw that more clearly than ever now.

Charles was waiting in the front hall when she came down the stairs. He looked distressed. He took the ring from her and turned it over in his palm.

"I'm sorry. I didn't want to hurt you. If you were still deaf, I wouldn't have deserted you."

"I know, Charles. You are a man of honor. You would have kept your promises to me, but this way is much better. Now we both are free. I wish you the best, Charles. Good-bye."

**21**

r. Grantly greeted her cordially. "I cannot tell you how glad I am at your remarkable recovery," he said, taking her hands.

He was visibly upset as she went on to tell him more about the Brimleys and how she and her fellow prisoners had been treated.

"I want to bring them all to justice. I intend to press assault charges. I hope that you will make some kind of statement or sign a document of some kind verifying that I *was* deaf. And that after that cruel blow, now I can hear."

Dr. Grantly fingered his gold watch chain and looked uncomfortable. "But I have no personal knowledge of that. I mean, of the man hitting you."

"But surely you agree that the kind of deafness such as mine, brought on by serious illness, may not always return spontaneously. And that a blow such as Brimley's could possibly bring it back."

"You mean you want me to testify to your condition before your abduction and give my professional opinion as a physician that your regained hearing could be the result of such a blow?"

"Yes, if you will. You see, it goes beyond just me and the way I was treated. There must be dozens of others disabled in various ways in the city of London who are right now being brutalized like I was. Like Alice, Mary, and the boys were by the Brimleys. The perpetrators should be punished. I have the means to pursue it legally, whereas those less financially fortunate than I could not. But I do need your support."

Dr. Grantly pursed his lips thoughtfully. "Yes, I could do that much. However, how does your grandmother feel about what you intend to do? It would mean publicity of a kind that she deplores."

"This has nothing to do with Grandmother. This is my challenge, my battle. What I've been through cannot be in vain, Dr. Grantly. I can't forget it and go on living as I lived before. I've been thinking of what I can do that would be positive. I want to turn Halcyon Court, the estate my father left me, into a boarding school for the underprivileged deaf where they can be taught lipreading or signing. Give their lives meaning and purpose. I think it's criminal the way such people are hidden away, ostracized for something that is not their fault, and given only the option to beg!" Paige was warming to her subject. She hadn't realized before how strongly she felt.

"Well, I commend you, my dear. It is an ambitious and worthy plan. And not without its challenges. I will do whatever I can to assist you." He picked up his medical bag and started toward the door. He put his hand on the knob, then turned back. "And what does the young lieutenant you're engaged to think of all this?"

"Charles? I didn't seek his opinion. This is my own idea, and I will carry it out by myself. We are no longer engaged."

"I see." Dr. Grantly paused. "More has changed than your ability to hear, I think."

Paige smiled. "Perhaps."

Dr. Grantly nodded, and Paige thought she saw a glimmer of approval in his eyes as he left the room.

He was right. Something had changed in her. For the better, she hoped. She felt a new kind of strength and determination.

Paige went upstairs, where she found Alice and Mary reading together cozily in front of the fireplace.

"Alice, I have a wonderful idea. I hope you will agree. How would you like to attend Alistair Sinclair's institute in Scotland and train to be a teacher of the deaf? You already know one system of signing, so that should qualify you as an applicant. And you have all the qualities that would make you an excellent teacher."

Alice was overjoyed at the idea. The two of them talked for the next hour about all the possibilities.

Things moved quickly after that. Paige contacted one of Mary's sisters, who was shocked to hear how her younger sister and the others had been treated. As Paige suspected, the Brimleys had shown them only the upper part of the house when the family had arranged for Mary to stay there. When Paige explained her plans for the school, Mary's sister enthusiastically agreed to allow Mary to accompany Alice to Scotland for training. Jeremy and Tom were already reunited with their parents and were on their way to a new missionary post.

All seemed to be going well when Paige received the worst news of her life.

Paige knew something was wrong when Flora, her eyes red and swollen, brought in her breakfast tray. Instead of the morning newspaper neatly folded beside the small pot of tea, Flora carried it under her arm. After setting the tray down on the table by the window, she stood uncertainly for a moment.

"What is it, Flora?" Paige asked.

"Oh, miss," she began, her mouth working, "I dinna know how to tell ye."

She handed Paige the paper. The headlines screamed: FREIGHTER LOST AT SEA—NO SURVIVORS.

Paige looked up at Flora, not registering the words. Then she let her eyes move down the page, scanning the article, until she saw the name *Star of India*—the cargo ship that belonged to the family's importing firm. The same one on which Thatcher had sailed to India and on which he would have returned to England.

Paige read the words out loud in horrified disbelief. "Cargo ship sinks in freak storm in the Arabian Sea. All crew and passengers believed drowned."

Thatcher gone. Dead! No, she couldn't bear it. Choking sobs rose in her throat. She flung down the paper and burst into a torrent of tears.

For two days Paige was inconsolable. She cried until it seemed no more tears were left. Grandmother, too, was devastated. Of the three children, Thatcher had always been Lady Ursula's favorite.

Paige couldn't eat. She couldn't sleep. All she could do was pace her room, sobbing. She knew Alice was distressed at her grief. She had often talked to her of Thatcher, her close childhood companion. Alice tried to comfort her, but it was no use. Paige felt such a well of sorrow within, nothing anyone could say could heal the wound.

Thatcher's loss was the third time Paige had lost someone important to her. First her beloved father, then her mother, and now her dearest friend. She felt abandoned and desolate.

Days went by—two—three—Paige was hardly aware of their passing. Finally, all emotions spent, she dragged herself back from the depths of sorrow. Somehow, she had to go on living. Thatcher would have wanted her to be brave. She could almost hear him saying, "Come on, Mopsy, chin up. Carry on." She had to do something worthwhile in her life, if for no other reason than to honor his trust in her.

Paige went ahead and made arrangements for Alice and Mary to go to the Sinclair Institute in Scotland. At the same time, word came that Basil Colfax had emigrated to Australia to avoid arrest. Presumably Helena and Demetra had accompanied him.

"Good-bye and good riddance," was Grandmother's terse comment. "From the first time he set foot in this house, Basil Colfax brought nothing but unhappiness and dissension into this family."

Paige struggled to forgive Demetra, who had, after all, been raised in an atmosphere of bitter resentment. She had coveted everything Paige had. Even, Paige suspected, Charles. In the end, however, she had left with nothing but a criminal reputation.

Well, it was all in the past now. Paige intended to look toward the future and make the most of all she was given to share with others.

*T*hree weeks later Paige saw Alice and Mary off to Scotland to take their training at the Sinclair Institute. Without them, Mallory Hall seemed lonely and very empty.

Lady Ursula also was gone, declaring the past winter had been altogether too much for her. She had left with her sister, Great-aunt Enid, on an extended tour of the resorts and spas recommended by Dr. Grantly as a restorative to body and spirit.

"At my age, it has all been much too much," she declared. "I shall sit in the sunshine in a bath chair and try to recover."

It was only after everyone had departed that the full sorrow of Thatcher's death came down upon Paige. Her dearest friend, her closest confidant from childhood, the person on whom she could always depend was lost to her forever.

Then it was spring again. Several months had passed since Paige's hearing had been restored, and the trial and conviction of the Brimleys were behind her. Now Paige decided to leave Mallory Hall and go down to Halcyon Court, where she had spent the happiest years of her life as a little girl. At Halcyon Court she hoped to find some solace for her spirit.

Halcyon Court was a rambling, stucco-and-timbered house where Queen Elizabeth and her courtiers had often been entertained by Mallory ancestors. Its acres of green rolling hills, stables, and farm had all been rescued by Paige's mother's fortune and were now part of *her* inheritance. She was working on a plan to make some additions in order to turn it into a boarding school for the hearing impaired. The residents would stay in the healthful countryside setting while learning either signing or lipreading or both, whichever form of communication would be best suited to their capabilities and degree of deafness.

A skeleton staff had stayed on through the years, so Paige took only Flora with her. She needed peace and quiet to reflect on all that had happened. Strangely enough, the breaking of her engagement to Charles had not made her as unhappy as it once might have. In fact, she felt freer than she ever had before. She knew it would never have been the ideal marriage she had at first imagined. Even with her restored hearing, they now had different values, different perspectives.

It was true that Paige had changed. She wasn't the person Charles had fallen in love with; her abduction and captivity had altered her perspective on life and deepened her faith. After Paige arrived at Halcyon Court, she began attending Sunday morning services at the village church. It was a lovely old Norman-style church built of weathered gray stone in the center of the small town across from the square of green. Adding to its beauty were the vines that climbed the ancient walls and turned crimson in the fall. The graveyard was off to one side, the headstones positioned tidily on the hillside beyond.

One particularly lovely Sunday after church Paige decided to dismiss her coachman and small buggy and walk back to Halcyon Court. As she strolled along, she breathed deeply of the fragrant fresh air. The evidence of spring was everywhere: filmy green buds on the trees, crocuses and daffodils pushing up through the thawing earth.

Her thoughts turned to Thatcher. At that part of this morning's service when individual prayer requests were taken, she had asked for the Prayer for Those Lost at Sea:

O Eternal God, who alone spreadest out the heavens, and rulest the raging of the sea: We commend to thy almighty protection, thy servant Thatcher, for whose preservation on the great deep our prayers are desired. Guard him, we beseech thee, from the dangers of the sea. Conduct him in safety to the haven where he would be, with a grateful sense of thy mercies; through Jesus Christ our Lord. Amen.

The beautiful words were comforting. Paige realized now that the same prayer could be applied to her. The Lord had watched over Alice and Paige, aided their escape, and freed the others from the Brimleys. She recalled the words of her governess, Miss Boles, so many years ago: "Adversity builds character. If it does not, it embitters and corrupts." Naturally Basil Colfax came to mind. How he had let misfortune corrupt him! And Demetra had been drawn into his plan of revenge. Even after all that her cousin had done, Paige hoped that somehow Demetra would find redemption.

Lost in thought, Paige was nearing the house when she saw the figure of a man approaching. Who could it be? Halcyon Court was quite a distance from the village, and none of the estate farmworkers or gardeners worked on Sunday.

Paige frowned. A stranger? She halted. There was something familiar about his walk. Her heart began to pound. Could it be? Of course not. As he came closer, she saw that he had a full beard and that his thick hair was bleached almost white with sun streaks.

Paige felt powerless to move. The man came nearer, and she saw a glimmer of white teeth as he smiled. Closer still, and she saw his eyes, curiously light blue in a deeply tanned face. She must be dreaming! Could it be? An answer to prayer?

*"Thatcher!"*

Even before this bearded stranger's identity was confirmed, Paige picked up her skirt and began to run toward him.

He stood waiting, arms outstretched. As she flung herself at him, he caught her up in a hug and swung her around twice before setting her back on her feet.

"Mopsy, dear old Mopsy!" He laughed.

"Am I dreaming?" Paige gasped. "Are you really here?"

"You're not, and I am." Thatcher said, laughing.

"We thought you were dead! We read about it in the papers. They said there were no survivors!"

Tears of joy were streaming down her face now. He wiped them away tenderly.

"I know, and I'm sorry." He nodded and to her amazement he repeated the words in sign language and continued to sign rapidly. *I went first to Mallory Hall and found Aunt Ursula is away, that she and Aunt Enid are in the south of France together. And Demetra is nowhere in sight. But Milton told me you had come down here to Halcyon Court. So I came straight away.*

Paige shook her head in disbelief. "I thought I was seeing a ghost!"

*I almost was a ghost!* Before she could tell him that she could now hear, Thatcher was signing again. He had an incredible story to tell. It soon became apparent to Paige that he had no idea what had happened to her since he'd received her last letter in which she had told him about her trip to Scotland to Alistair Sinclair's clinic. She had enclosed one of the illustrated instruction books on his method of signing. Evidently Thatcher had been studying it ever since.

*I was determined to learn signing so that when I got back we would have no trouble communicating and understanding each other. When I completed my business at the company's office in Calcutta, I was eager to get home. I boarded our ship the* Star of India, *only taking a few passengers. It was slow, and knowing you would be gone six weeks or more, I was in no real hurry to get home. The fact that I was homeward bound was enough. As we ploughed our slow way from the coast into the*

*Arabian Sea, I spent my days on deck reading and studying signing.* Thatcher grinned. *And getting pretty proficient in it, wouldn't you say?*

At this compassionate gesture of affection Paige felt a lump rise in her throat. That Thatcher had cared this much about her deeply touched her. She wanted him to have this moment of triumph before telling him her hearing had been restored.

"Well, you certainly are, Thatcher, I can understand you perfectly."

*Good.* His smile broadened. *If I hadn't been so occupied, the days might have been monotonous indeed. It was very hot, and actually being on deck was preferable to being in my cramped cabin. That fateful night I was sitting up on deck, it was so hot, and everything seemed very still—unnaturally so. The clouds blacked out the stars I'd seen on other nights, and in the distance we saw lightning flashes.*

*That night I had no premonition, none at all. After dinner I took a stroll on deck, standing at the rail for a few minutes watching the streaks of lightning zigzagging across the sky. Then I went to my cabin, where I read until I fell asleep.*

*I could not have been asleep more than a couple of hours when I was awakened by a crash of thunder. A sudden lurch threw me out of my bunk onto the floor. Lightning coming in flash after flash made the cabin as bright as day. The ship was rocking like crazy. I staggered to my feet, pulled my trousers on over my nightshirt, grabbed my jacket, slipped it on, and for some reason—heaven knows—I stuffed the signing booklet in my jacket, along with my New Testament—you remember the one Miss Boles gave each of us before she left the year I went off to boarding school?*

Paige nodded. She still had hers too. She felt a pang of guilt—until a few months ago she had read far too little of it.

Thatcher went on with his exciting story. *I yanked open the door and went out into the passageway. The few other passengers crowded into the narrow space, all making for the ladder to get up on deck. The wind was howling—like a thousand wolves. The ship was rolling sideways, and waves were sweeping over the rail and swirling onto the deck.* Thatcher waved his arms in exaggerated circles as he described the violence of the storm at sea.

"I think I am so overwhelmed that I feel weak!" she laughed. "Come let us sit down, and you must tell me the rest."

They walked to one of the several wrought iron benches overlooking the terraced lawns and lily pond. There Thatcher continued his story.

At this point Paige couldn't prolong Thatcher's tremendous effort to relay his long story in sign language any longer. She held up her hand.

"Wait, Thatcher. Before you go on, I have something important to tell you. I can hear. A few months ago my hearing was restored."

His expression underwent a rapid change—from disbelief to uncertainty, then to elation.

"When? How? That's wonderful!" His grin was wide and as joyous as a boy's. He came closer and hugged her. "Good girl! My own Mopsy, you did it! I knew if anyone could, *you* could." He whirled her around once or twice. "I could dance a jig! In fact, I *can* dance one. I learned how from the ship's Irish cook." He took her arm and twirled her around, then hugged her again. "Tell me all about it, Paige. I imagine Charles is over the moon about it."

Paige looked at him directly. "Charles isn't in the picture anymore, Thatcher. But that is another story."

Thatcher looked puzzled, and to delay his questions, Paige slipped her hand through his arm and urged, "Let's go up to the house where we can be more comfortable. I'll tell you everything, but first finish about the shipwreck and how you survived. My story can wait."

"Well," he continued, "it was soon apparent from the force of the wind and the waves and the creaking and cracking of the ship that it might not ride out the storm. I confess I was alarmed, to put it mildly. I saw the fear in the eyes of the seasoned sailors, and when I saw one washed overboard right in front of my eyes, I realized my own life was in danger. The deck was a madhouse. No heroes that I saw. People yelling and screaming, the captain shouting orders at the crew, who didn't seem to be paying attention, everyone scrambling into the available lifeboats. When I saw the bedlam, I decided I'd better take my chances rather than fight for a place on one of the lifeboats that were probably already doomed by over-crowding and inexperienced boatsmen. Panic does queer things to folks. I saw a life preserver hanging on the railing and headed toward it. Just as I got the canvas ring over one arm, a huge wave rushed over the listing side and knocked me off my feet. I fell flat on my face on the deck, and the next thing I knew I was swept over the side with the receding wave down and into the water. Although I was plunged deep into the waves and had to battle my way to the surface, thank God, somehow I held fast to the life preserver. I don't know how many hours I battled the churning waves. I was only half-conscious part of the time. Around me I could hear the voices, moans, and cries of others who must have survived the actual sink-ing of our ship. My eyes were stinging from salt water; I was nauseous from swallowing so much. It was pitch dark, and I floated thinking every minute might be my last."

"Oh, Thatcher, how brave you were!"

"Not brave, just desperate. I realized how much I wanted to live, how much I wanted to get back to England. I couldn't bear the thought of never seeing you or anyone I loved again. I must have become unconscious for a while. Finally dawn came. I was grateful I had lasted the night. Then suddenly I realized I was drifting not against the waves but with them. I managed to raise my head and squint into the distance, and then I saw—I can't tell you the emotions that surged up in me—a ridge of sand, a few palm trees, land, an island!"

Paige squeezed his hand.

"I looked around me. I saw a few pieces of wood, debris from the ship, but no people. Except one head bobbing not too far away. A voice called, 'Ahoy there, matey.' I twisted my head and saw an arm waving, a wrinkled face—the two of us were the only survivors."

"What a miracle, Thatcher."

"Yes, it was just that. I was to find out how much of a miracle in the next few weeks when we were stranded on the island."

"Did you know him?"

"No, as the ship's cook he never came in contact with the passengers. He was an excellent cook. And what he did with what little we found to eat on the island was also a miracle. If you have to be shipwrecked with someone, I can recommend a cook as first choice." Thatcher laughed.

Paige joined in the laughter. How wonderful it was for the two of them to be laughing together again!

"His name was O'Rourke, and cooking wasn't his only expertise. Would you believe he was a Shakespeare scholar and a Bible reader as well?"

"That's too much!"

"But absolutely true. It saved us both, believe me. And when he saw my New Testament and the instruction book for signing, soggy and waterlogged, he exclaimed 'Praise the Lord!' We spent many an hour trying to best each other with quotations from the Bard's plays and the verses of Bible chapters we remembered."

"And how were you rescued?"

"We tried to keep some kind of log of the time we were there, but that was hard. One day was very much the same as the one before. Our first days were spent in the search for food and water. When we had regained our strength a little, we hiked back into the hills to look for some sort of spring. Again, by God's grace, we found a pool and were able to drink crystal-clear water. Nothing ever tasted so good! You know, a man can survive without food longer than without water. O'Rourke even conducted an impromptu thanksgiving service right there. Every night we built a bonfire from driftwood and dried palm leaves and anything else we could find, hoping some passing ship would see it and come to investigate. Not only hoping but praying. Eventually one did."

"It's a wonder you were ever found. I shall never forget the headlines the London newspaper printed: FREIGHTER LOST AT SEA—NO SURVIVORS. I was devastated."

"Poor Mopsy." Thatcher looked at her fondly. "But here I am back like a bad penny." He paused. "Now, I want to hear about you and your recovery. Your last letter was full of your excitement about going to Alistair Sinclair's clinic, and obviously that was—"

"There's a great deal more to add to that. But let's go inside; we'll have some tea, and I will tell you all about my adventure."

Arms around each other's waists, they walked back up the rest of the driveway toward the house together.

Thatcher had never been at Halcyon Court. Stepping inside the massive carved doors, he glanced all around the paneled entry. He followed Paige through the double doors leading into the drawing room. Floor-length windows overlooking the gardens shed sunlight on the worn oak floors.

After Paige rang for tea to be brought, they settled into the curved sofa in front of the large stone fireplace where a fire glowed.

"Now about *you!*" Thatcher ordered. "Tell me everything."

For the next two hours Paige told Thatcher the whole complicated story of her abduction, her time at the Brimleys', and her discovery of how Demetra was involved in all of it.

When she had completed her tale, Thatcher shook his head. He got up from the sofa and paced the length of the carpet, hands clenched behind his back. "Who would have ever guessed our little Milquetoast of a cousin was behind all your misery?"

"I've had to forgive her, Thatcher. She was a pawn of her father, fed for years on his resentment and bitterness. I seemed to have so much, she so little." Paige paused, "Anyway, something good has come of it all." She went on to tell him about

Alice and Mary and her plans for the boarding school for the deaf.

As the afternoon wore on, they seemed to have more and more to talk about, more to share.

"I think you're much too forgiving," Thatcher said at one point.

"But there was much in me that needed forgiving as well. I can understand why Demetra envied me. I was thoughtless, self-absorbed with my own happiness, with Charles—"

"About Charles," Thatcher interrupted. "You said he was no longer in the picture. What does that mean? Is he stationed elsewhere on assignment?"

Briefly Paige told him that part of her story, then added, "He will be far happier with someone else. Someone more suited to be an army officer's wife than I."

"There is no one better suited to be a wife," Thatcher contradicted her statement.

Paige looked at him quizzically and went on, "Oh, well, it is all in the past now. Let me tell you what I plan to do . . ."

With enthusiasm she plunged into the details of her plans. When she finished, Thatcher leaned forward and took both her hands in his. "What can I do to help?" he asked. "Is there a place for me in your plans—in your life?"

Paige halted midsentence, forgetting what it was she was about to say. She found herself lost in Thatcher's gaze.

Paige looked at Thatcher and saw beyond the beard and shaggy hair. There were new lines that gave his face a maturity that had not been there before. Of course, he had retained his old sense of humor, yet his eyes had a subtle depth now that only his incredible testing and subsequent survival could have placed there. Whatever pain and suffering he had endured had given him a strength that made him even more handsome. Character was indelibly etched on his face.

Her heart warmed at his spontaneous offer. To help, to be a part of her plans, a part of her future?

She would not have expected less from his generous nature. But there was something new and vibrant trembling between them. The person she had always cared for with affection now evoked something deeper. He held her hands captured in his, then he leaned forward and they kissed.

The kiss was not a cousinly kiss but a lover's kiss. When it ended, Thatcher put his hands on either side of her face and looked deeply into her eyes, searching for an answer to an unspoken question. When he spoke his voice was low, husky with emotion.

"Paige, I have loved you for so long. Just about the time I had worked up enough courage to tell you so, Charles came into your life. And it was obvious right from the first that you were smitten. I thought it meant your happiness, and I wanted you to have all you deserved—"

Paige put her fingertips on his lips. "No, no, Thatcher, I didn't deserve anything. I was a shallow girl who fell in love with a handsome uniform. You were so right when you called him my 'toy soldier,' but actually it was I who was a puppet dancing to the tune of foolish dreams. There was nothing real about me, nothing to love."

He kissed her again. "It doesn't matter about the past, darling. We have the future to think about. All that we shall do together. For the rest of our lives."

Paige closed her eyes, feeling all the anxiety of the past months fade. She realized that all she had ever longed for, all she had missed, all she had thought lost forever was being restored in this moment.

"Yes," Paige whispered. Yes to all that was to come, to all they would find together.